The Wedding PARTY

a **HOLLYWOOD** *&Vine* novella

OLIVIA EVANS

ISBN-13: 978-1727367201

Editor: Lisa A. Hollett, Silently Correcting Your Grammar, LLC
Cover Designer: Jada D'Lee Designs
Interior Design and Formatting: Jill, Evil Kitty Books

For everyone who waited 84 years for me to publish this book.
You guys rock.

Chapter One

ON THE SECOND FLOOR OF an exclusive resort hotel in Fiji, guests filed into a private room. Caterers bustled around them, carrying trays of brunch appetizers and filling glasses with champagne or rum punch. At the back of the room, Anders leaned against the wall. Beside him, white curtains billowed in the breeze. The floor-to-ceiling windows were open wide, allowing the smell of sand and salt to flood the room. The sound of waves crashing onto the beach echoed in the distance.

He moved his eyes over the room, watching as people chatted in small groups, their smiles wide and their eyes filled with excitement. He found Josie standing with her best friends, Madison and Chloe, her head thrown back in laughter, a glass clutched in her hand. His eyes traveled along the slope of her nose to the pout of her lips before dropping lower to the swell of her breasts. A small smile lifted one side of his mouth even as his body tensed, overcome with emotion. He wondered if this was how she'd felt that first night. The night she'd planned to have a reckless one-night stand.

Anders shook his head and pushed off the wall as he made his way toward her. He'd thought the same thing at the time. How wonderfully wrong they'd been. Stepping up beside her, he slid his arm around her waist, flexing his fingers into her side.

"Hey," he exhaled against her skin, chuckling when she shivered and turned to face him. Her crystal-blue eyes shone with mirth as she wrapped her arms around his neck.

"Hey yourself," she murmured, her gaze focused on his lips.

Anders leaned forward, his lips brushing against her ear. "If you don't stop looking at me like that, we're going to have to find an office with a sturdy wall."

"Behave," Josie laughed, giving him a quick kiss before spinning out of his arms and grabbing his hand.

He allowed her to pull him to the same spot where he'd been watching her earlier, all hope of finding an empty office for a little wall sex vanishing when another group of people walked into the room.

"I don't know if I'm ready for this," Anders groaned, his gaze sweeping around the room again. Beside him, Josie tensed. When he saw the look of apprehension on her face, he rolled his eyes.

"Not *this*," he said, motioning between them with an expression that all but called her crazy. He sent a pointed stare toward the crowd before meeting Josie's gaze once more. "That."

Josie furrowed her brows. "Well, I'm not asking you to marry any of them—only me."

"Always the smartass," he chuckled, pulling her tighter against his side. "What I mean is, I don't know if I can handle all these people at the same time. One-on-one, I'm fine...ish, but beyond that...well, I don't enjoy hanging with people I mostly think are idiots. And let's be real, Ivy. There are a lot of idiots here."

Josie grinned and wrapped her arms around his waist. "You'll be fine. The guys have all sorts of fun things planned."

Anders scrunched up his face, his stormy blue eyes revealing every ounce of disdain he felt. He'd much rather be locked away in their villa having his way with her. "Do I look like a fucking five-year-old? I don't need group activities. All I need is alcohol and air conditioning."

"You're so high-maintenance," Josie sighed, draining the rest of her punch. "Just let me do the talking for now. You stand there and be pretty."

Anders smirked. "You want me to be your arm candy?"

"Can you think of any other reason I'd put up with you?"

Anders leaned closer, brushing his fingers along the underside of her breast as he spoke. "I'm sure I can think of a few."

"Anders," Josie whispered in what he assumed was her pathetic attempt at scolding him. She was well on her way to a good buzz. It wouldn't take much more to convince her to sneak away.

"If you expect me to believe you're not interested, maybe you shouldn't say my name in the same tone you do when my tongue—"

"Get a room!"

Anders released a harsh breath before turning to where Madison stood with a huge smile stretched across her face. One side of his mouth lifted into a devious smile, and his brow rose in amusement. "As a matter of fact, we happen to have one of those. I was just telling Josie about the things I planned to—"

"Mom! Dad! You're here!" Josie yelled, her eyes wide as she jammed her elbow into Anders's side.

"Fuck," he whispered while shifting his weight, his mischief set aside. He didn't know what it was about Josie's dad that unnerved him so much, but never in his life had anyone intimidated him more. Anders shook his head. That was a complete lie. He knew exactly why that man freaked him the fuck out.

The first time they'd met, Josie's dad had shown Anders his "war room," as he called it. Turned out, Josie's dad was a retired Navy SEAL sniper. A detail she'd conveniently left out.

Anders felt Josie's hand skim up his back. When he looked over his shoulder at her, the amusement on her face caused his lips to press into a thin line. "Don't worry," she whispered. "Mom made him leave his guns at home."

"I'm still pissed at you for not telling me about him. You know that, right?"

Josie laughed. "That was almost two years ago! How can you still be mad?"

Anders shrugged. "Holding grudges is kind of my thing."

"I think," Josie whispered, hugging him from behind, "you just like to bring it up because I always apologize in a very special way."

A smile tugged at the corner of Anders's mouth as he thought about the way she'd apologized that night and every other time the subject came up. He couldn't help but wonder why he didn't bring it up more. "Well, now that you mention it…" He turned to face her, making sure she felt his implication.

"I swear we're going to have to hose you two off."

Josie laughed, and Anders swore under his breath as he turned to Josie's mother and gave her a stiff smile. "Mrs. Bane," he coughed, his voice strained.

She waved him off and pulled him into a hug. Anders made sure to keep their lower bodies apart. The last thing he wanted was for his future mother-in-law to feel his erection. "I hope you put all this sexual tension to good use and give me a grandbaby soon." Anders choked on a gasp of air at her whispered words. Josie's mom pulled back and smiled, her face not giving away the fact that she'd just called Anders out for having a hard-on. "I've told you to call me Sonya."

Anders coughed and nodded, his eyes darting around the room, unable to make eye contact with Sonya. Josie's parents were fucking insane.

"Mom, are you hitting on my fiancé again?" Josie asked. Anders shook his head.

"Of course," she answered at the same time Anders said, "Of course not."

Josie laughed. "Mom, this is why I don't invite you to visit more."

"Is your mother hitting on Anders again?" Josie's dad asked, causing Anders to drop his chin to his chest and sigh. Her dad laughed and clapped Anders on the shoulder. "Don't worry, son. I left my guns at home."

"Dad," Josie admonished even though Anders could hear the laughter in her voice.

Pulling in a deep breath, Anders lifted his head and extended his hand. "Keith, it's good to see you." He knew better than to call him Mr. Bane; he'd learned that lesson early on. Josie's father gave him an approving smile.

"Good to see you, son. Are you ready for what we have planned today?"

Anders swallowed and looked from Josie to her father then to her brother Holden, who stood nearby with a wide smile that clearly conveyed Anders was most certainly not ready for what they had planned. "Yup."

"If I could have everyone's attention," Josie called, pulling Anders from the seventh circle of Bane hell. "I just want to thank you all for coming. I can't tell you what it means to Anders and me that you all took time out of your busy lives to share this special time with us."

"We paid for it. What do they care?" Anders muttered, leading Josie to give him one of her top ten bitch faces.

Anders shoved his hands into his pockets and let his gaze drift over the people gathered in front of him. Holden and Maddie stood next to Chloe and her boyfriend Reid, their expressions ranging from amused to sympathetic. Beside them were Anders's friends from LA, Owen and Walker, his agent, Nathan, with his wife, Elizabeth, Inky and Greer from Reid's band, Chloe's mother, and some chick named Lori who worked with Josie. It was going to be a small wedding. Anders didn't want a big show of fake-ass people coming to their wedding for the sake of being seen.

That was especially true when it came to his parents.

These were people who were important to Josie and Anders. They were people who didn't expect anything. For the longest time, he'd only had Nathan, Owen, and Walker—when he wasn't in rehab. Now though, there were others, and not because they had to be there or because they served a purpose. They were in his life because of Josie, and if he was honest, because he wanted them there.

Fuck, he was turning into a pussy. He'd make a point to piss them off at some point just to keep things in perspective. The thought made him smile. Not because he wanted to make them mad, but because Josie would be mad as hell, and they'd have killer angry sex.

"Stop thinking about sex," Josie hissed.

Anders chuckled. "You might as well tell me to stop breathing."

"Jesus," Josie exhaled. "We're going to have lots of angry sex this weekend, aren't we?"

"Damn straight."

"You realize we're still standing here," Keith said, causing Anders and Josie to laugh.

"Hush," Sonya said. "All this sexual tension will lead to babies. Just let it happen."

"Oh God," Josie groaned as a warm feeling mixed with a heavy dose of nausea washed over Anders. He'd never given much thought to children, but suddenly the image of Josie, her belly swollen with their child, made a lump form in his throat. He wasn't sure if it was desire or fear, but it was definitely something to ponder later—when her father wasn't giving him a death glare and her mom wasn't looking at him like she was willing to be impregnated.

"Anyway," Anders said, clapping his hands together. "We're going to do some dumb shit, drink too much, and regret most of what happens over the next four days, so you fuckers might as well prepare yourselves. That being said, I want to make it perfectly fucking clear that if any of you ruins a single moment of this for my girl, I'll fucking kill you. Thanks for coming. Let's get this shitshow on the road."

Next to him, Josie gasped, her mouth hanging open and her eyes wide. "Anders!"

He shrugged, his brows raised and his expression conveying that he didn't give a single shit if he'd offended anyone. "Ivy," he said, his tone matching his expression. "This is our wedding. We paid for all these assholes to be here, even though some of them have more money than I do. The least they can do is not fuck up our wedding. Am I right?"

"He is right, baby girl," Keith said, stepping next to Anders.

"Although he could have delivered the message with a little more finesse, I think we'd be pushing it to ask for more than we got. In his own way, that was his effort to tell people not to fuck up your big day. You can't be mad at the guy for that."

"Did you just say fuck?" Josie whispered, her eyes widening when her mother wrapped her arms around her dad and winked.

"You should hear him—"

"Okay, Mom, that's enough out of you," Holden said, coming to stand next to her and pulling her almost-empty drink from her hand. Anders and Josie exhaled in relief as her dad smirked. Anders shook his head. He'd said it once, and he'd say it again: Josie's parents were fucking insane.

"Are you ready for today?" Holden asked.

Anders narrowed his eyes as he looked between Keith and Holden. "That depends on what you guys have planned." The truth was, he already knew, thanks to Reid, but they didn't need to know that.

Holden laughed. "It'll be fun, don't worry. Although you might want to change before we go."

Anders looked down at his slacks and button-down shirt. He knew he needed to change, but he might as well have a little fun playing dumb. "What's wrong with what I'm wearing?"

Holden rolled his eyes. "Did you bring shorts?"

Anders scoffed. He wasn't that uptight. Anymore. "Of course, I did. I have several pairs of athletic shorts."

"And I assume you have T-shirts to go with those shorts?"

"Yes," Anders answered with his own eye roll. Holden was totally busting his balls.

"Awesome. Put those on with a pair of sneakers and meet us out front in twenty minutes. And make sure whatever you put on isn't expensive. It will likely be ruined by the time we get back."

Holden and Keith turned away, yelling for the others, to give them the same instructions they'd given Anders. Anders turned to Josie. "What the fuck have I gotten myself into?"

"You'll be fine."

"You're so full of shit. I can see it all over your face."

Josie laughed, her eyes darting around the room. "Okay, I have no idea if you'll be fine, but I can promise they won't kill you. That's something, yeah?"

Anders shook his head, amused. "You're as bad as the rest of them. Away with you, she-witch. Have fun with your mom bringing up my dick impregnating you for the rest of the night. Rum punch is at least on my side for now."

"Fuck," Josie whispered, her cheeks pinking. "I'm going to have to cut her off. She's out of control."

Anders laughed. "Good luck with that, Ivy. I'll see you later."

Josie frowned and rocked up on her toes to give Anders a quick kiss. "This was such a bad idea."

"Horrible."

"What were we thinking?"

"I have no idea, but it's too late now. Good luck to us both."

Josie sighed. "Be careful, Asshole."

Anders chuckled and pulled Josie against him, his lips lingering on her forehead. "You too, Ivy."

With a deep breath, Anders headed toward their villa to change clothes before subjecting himself to an afternoon in the jungle.

9

Chapter Two

UNDER THE BLISTERING SUN, ANDERS stared at the four-wheeled death machine before glancing at his friends. Owen and Walker were fucked. "Someone is going to die."

Holden laughed and handed Anders a helmet. "You'll be fine, I swear. My dad used to take me on these things all the time. You have nothing to worry about."

"This is bullshit," Owen said, his face twisted with disdain. "We have stunt doubles to do this shit for us. I can't afford to wreck one of these. What if I mess up my face? Or end up paralyzed? What happened to a good ole strip club and booze?"

"And a little bit of coke," Walker added, earning a disapproving glare from Anders. "We're not cut out for this shit, Anders."

"I have my camera ready," Reid whispered, his eyes on Owen and Walker as he moved beside Anders. "These are just like the ones we rented last weekend. Steer clear of those two, and you'll be fine."

Anders looked at Reid and grinned. "Thanks for the heads-up. At least now I have a chance of not crashing into a tree." Anders chuckled when Walker swore as he climbed onto the four-wheeler. "Please tell me you plan to ride behind him and Owen. It would be a shame not to get this on video."

"Damn straight, I am," Reid laughed, clapping Anders on the back as he and Greer climbed onto their four-wheelers.

Anders wasn't sure how it had happened, but Reid had somehow become his closest friend over the last year. Sure, he was still tight with Owen and Walker—well, as close as anyone could be to those two. But they still lived like bachelors, and as cool as Josie was about a lot of things, having half-naked women hanging all over him wasn't one of them. While his relationship with Holden was definitely better, Anders knew he'd never come before Josie, and that put a barrier between them that would never diminish.

"Man the fuck up, assholes. Let's roll." Anders climbed onto the four-wheeler, making sure to keep his expression neutral when he noticed the smirks Holden and Keith wore. The half-day trip had been their idea. The plan was to ride inland, then have a short exploration of Naihehe Cave. After, they'd go back to the resort and drink on the beach. He was certain Holden and Keith had picked this particular excursion to get a few laughs at Anders's expense, but the joke was on them. He'd need to buy Reid a new guitar for this one.

It took less than an hour for things to go south. "Shit!" Owen yelled as he dodged a tree branch. He hadn't been so lucky the time before; the bright red mark on his face was proof of that. Anders had nearly hit a tree when it happened because he couldn't stop laughing.

"Anders, I'm going to kick your ass!"

"You can't even stay on the path!" Anders yelled. "You might want to concentrate more on not dying and less on trying to kick my ass."

"Your face is fucked, man," Walker said to Owen as he moved closer to Anders.

Wary of Walker's driving, Anders eased toward the path's edge. He looked in Walker's direction to gauge their distance, his eyes widening at what he saw. "Look out!"

Anders's warning came at the same moment the front of Walker's four-wheeler dropped, sending him flying over the handlebars. Walker sailed through the air before landing flat on his back in the middle of the trail. The group slammed on their brakes and jumped down, rushing to where he lay motionless.

"Walker." Nathan hovered above him, quickly followed by Anders, Reid, and the rest of the group. Walker sucked in a few short breaths before his chest finally expanded with a lungful of air. Anders shook his head as he reached down and helped Walker to his feet. As funny as it was seeing Walker fly through the air ass over feet, he couldn't help but think how easily that could have been him had Reid not taken him for lessons.

"Are you okay?" Nathan asked, his expression full of concern.

Walker shook his head and waved for everyone to get back. "Jesus," he gasped, pulling in another gulp of air. After several deep breaths, he looked at Anders, his eyes narrowed. "Tell me again why we couldn't do normal shit like strippers and drugs for your bachelor party?"

Anders chuckled and pulled Walker to his feet. "Because Josie would have my balls in a vise."

Walker grumbled and wiped the back of his shorts clean before walking back to the four-wheeler. Anders looked away, trying to hide his laugh when his eyes landed on Nathan, whose face was bright with amusement.

"Remember that one time you said you wanted to do your own stunts?" Nathan asked. "Think about this the next time you have another idea like that."

The memory made Anders grimace. "I damn sure dodged a bullet there. I can't believe people do shit like this voluntarily. What kind of maniacs do we work with?"

Nathan chuckled and adjusted his helmet. "The kind that actually goes to their training sessions."

Not wanting to argue with Nathan for the hundredth time about his less-than-perfect attendance to his sessions, Anders adjusted his helmet and started up his four-wheeler. The smell of dust and gas burned his nose as the group continued toward the village closest to the cave's entrance, this time at a much slower pace.

Thick vegetation surrounded them, bright green moss-covered rocks, tree trunks, and everything in between. Small animals scurried to safety as the line of four-wheelers made their way to a small village hidden in the middle of the island. As they'd been instructed when leaving the resort, they drove to the house at the end of the street surrounded by a wire fence, a large wooden arbor-like structure in the front.

"Where the hell are we?" Owen whispered, his eyes moving over the people in front of the house, who stared at the group with mild curiosity.

Anders shook his head, his brows pulled low as the group climbed off their ATVs and removed their helmets. "How the fuck should I know? I didn't plan this train wreck."

"I swear to God, Anders, if they want a sacrifice or some shit, I nominate your brother-in-law," Walker whispered, moving to Anders's other side.

Anders looked from Owen to Walker, his expression incredulous. "Are you both high?"

Owen laughed. "I can't speak for Mr. Rehab over there, but I'm straight as an arrow."

"Seriously, though," Reid said, joining the others. "What are we doing here?"

"It's some sort of ritual we have to do before we're allowed to enter the cave. This is where the priest lives. We'll eat, he'll bless us, then we can swim." Everyone looked at Nathan like he had two heads. He shrugged. "I took the time to look this stuff up before we left."

"Look it up? How did you know what they had planned?"

Nathan laughed and clapped Anders on the back. "I helped plan everything."

"Traitor," Anders muttered as everyone followed Nathan to where Holden and Keith stood with a group of locals. After everyone shook hands and sized each other up, they made their way inside the house.

Wood carvings and paintings covered the walls of the small house. Knickknacks littered the tops of every surface, most appearing to be handmade. Anders dropped his eyes to the scuffed wooden floor, watching as their steps caused the layer of dirt to swirl into the air. Filing in the dining room, the group took their places around a large table. Reid moved next to Anders and bumped his shoulder. "This should be interesting."

Anders's brows furrowed then relaxed as he followed Reid's line of sight. Walker, Owen, and Greer were on the other side of the room, chatting with a couple of girls who couldn't have seemed more disinterested. Behind them were two guys who were obviously the girls' boyfriends.

Anders smirked. "Twenty bucks they get their asses kicked before we sit down to eat."

Reid laughed. "I'm not taking that bet. They're totally going to get their asses kicked."

Anders nodded. "Can't blame a guy for trying to make a

quick buck. Let's move closer so we can actually hear them crash and burn."

With their hands shoved into the pockets of their shorts, the pair moved closer to where Owen, Walker, and Greer were obviously making fools of themselves.

"You can't be serious," Owen said. The look of disbelief on his face was comical.

The girl in front of him shrugged. "Are we supposed to know who you guys are?"

"Well, yeah," Walker said like it was the most obvious thing.

"Should we apologize?" the other girl asked, her words weighted with restrained laughter. Anders had a feeling those girls knew exactly who Walker and Owen were but had no intention of letting them know.

"We know who you are," Girl Number One said with a smile as she looked at Anders. He couldn't have stopped the smirk that stretched across his face if he'd wanted to, not that he'd ever want to in the first place.

"Sorry, guys," Anders chuckled, but before he could gloat further, the girl spoke again.

"You're the groom. Congratulations, by the way!"

Next to him, Reid coughed into his hand in a pathetic attempt to hide his laughter. Anders pursed his lips and cut his eyes to Reid. "I don't see them throwing their panties at you either, Mr. Rock Star. Looks like you're as unknown as the rest of us."

"Not true," Girl Number One sang, her fingers laced in front of her, a shy smile on her lips. "You're Reid Ryder." Tipping her chin to the other side of Reid, she continued. "And you're Greer Lawson. We're big fans." Greer winked at the girls, eliciting a giggle from them, while Anders, Owen, and Walker rolled their eyes.

"Now I know they're fucking with us," Owen grumbled.

Anders chuckled. "Probably, but you two are the only ones who care."

"Do you guys want a drink?"

Anders jumped at the sound of the unfamiliar voice, his eyes landing on one of the two guys standing behind the girls. He'd forgotten they were there, and from the looks on their faces, they weren't very pleased about that oversight.

"A drink sounds like a great idea," Reid said, clapping Anders on the shoulder. "We're here to celebrate this guy getting married, after all."

Reid's wide smile and friendly voice made it clear to Anders that Reid was trying to calm what any idiot could see was the beginning of a very strained situation. Well, any idiot who wasn't named Walker Hayes; he was completely fucking oblivious.

The guy smiled, seemingly appeased by Reid's friendly disposition. "You guys have a seat. We'll grab some punch."

"So what tortures do you guys have planned after this?" Anders asked as everyone found a seat at the table.

Keith, Holden, and Nathan laughed. "I promise the rest should be fairly tame. Once we eat and have the priest's blessing, we'll go down to the cave. We can swim or do a little exploring, whatever you're up for. After that, we'll pack everything up and head back to the resort," Keith said, nodding in thanks as a drink and a small plate of food were placed in front of him.

"Then the real party can start," Owen said, raising his glass in cheers. Anders couldn't help but agree as he raised his own glass.

For the next half hour, they ate lunch while chatting with

their hosts. Once the table had been cleared, the priest, along with a few of his family members, accompanied the group to the mouth of the cave where the blessing ceremony was performed. It took less than five minutes, and while Anders didn't understand half of what was said, he couldn't help but have respect for their culture.

"What is that?" Walker asked, his voice barely above a whisper. Anders blinked and looked from Walker to where he pointed by the cave. The heat from the sun made the air shimmer, and the rocks almost appeared to be dancing. Anders shook his head, certain his eyes were playing tricks on him.

"It's nothing. Come on, let's move inside. It's hot as fuck out here. I want to swim." He took a step forward and stumbled. "The fuck?"

"Dude, is it just me, or is the water singing?"

Anders looked at Greer like he'd grown a second head. "Are you high?"

Greer shook his head and swallowed. "Nah, man. I'm just hot. I think you're right. We should go swim."

"What's wrong with you?" Nathan asked, moving next to Anders.

"I'm fine. Let's go."

One by one, the guys filed into the cave, some steadier than others. Once they'd shed their shirts and shoes, Reid, Anders, and Greer dove into the cool water.

"I think they spiked our drinks," Reid said, his eyes darting around the cave. "It's either that or I have a brain tumor."

Anders laughed, a wave of euphoria washing over him. He lifted his hand out of the water and turned it from side to side. "The water's thick."

Greer gasped and lifted his hand out of the water just as Anders had done. "It is," he whispered, his voice filled with awe.

For a brief moment, the trio was silent, hypnotized by the water around them. Then the screaming started. It was high-pitched, ear-shattering, and terror-inducing.

"Bat! Bat! We're all going to die!" Walker screamed, his eyes wide as he flailed his arms in the air, fighting off an attacker only he could see.

"Get out of the water!" Nathan yelled. "Anders, do you hear me? Get out of the water!"

"What's in the water?" Reid choked, splashing around. "Is it a snake? A crocodile? Is something going to eat us?"

Panic began to work its way through Anders as shadows took shape and moved closer. "What the fuck is happening?"

A loud splash by the rocks caused the three guys to jump and kick away from whatever was moving toward them. "I can't die. Josie will be so pissed."

"Then I suppose you'd better get out of the water before you drown," Holden said, tugging on Anders's arm. "Come on, all of you."

Walker continued to scream and fight off the bats as Holden and Keith helped Anders, Reid, and Greer out of the water. Huddled together, they sat with their arms wrapped around their legs and rocked back and forth.

"What did you find out?" Keith asked, his eyes focused on Nathan.

"They'll be fine," Nathan sighed, taking a look at his watch. "In about three more hours."

"What happens in three hours?" Greer whispered. "They're going to sacrifice us to the cave gods, aren't they? I'd be a terrible sacrifice! Tell them! Do you have any idea how many bad things I've done? They'll be cursed forever."

Nathan groaned. "There are no cave gods, and no one is sacrificing anyone. In three hours, you'll be good as new."

"How do you know?" Anders asked, his eyes fixed on Walker as Holden struggled to keep him from punching a rock he swore was a large killer bat.

"Because that's when the shrooms will wear off."

"Shrooms," Keith muttered, nodding. "Of course. Any idea why?"

"The guys back at the house thought it would be funny. They knew who we were. I'm sure the fact that Owen, Walker, and Greer were flirting with their girlfriends didn't help either."

"Jesus."

Greer looked from side to side. "Where is Owen? Has anybody seen Owen? They sure as hell don't want to use him for a sacrifice. He's worse than all of us!"

Nathan sighed. "I told you no one is being sacrificed, Greer. And Owen is fine."

"Where is he?" Keith whispered to Nathan.

"He's tucked away in a little hole by the entrance with what I'm praying is mud smeared all over him," Nathan answered, trying to keep a straight face. "He's also naked, which is why I thought it would be best to leave him where he is."

Anders scrubbed his hands over his face. "This is so fucked up," he muttered before closing his eyes and willing the flying snakes to disappear.

As Nathan promised, three hours later, the world began to return to normal. What transpired during that time was something none of them wanted to talk about ever again, but no one less than Owen.

Once everyone was dressed and seated on their four-wheelers, Owen looked around the group, traces of mud still smeared on his face and neck. "Not a word about this. Ever. Let's get the hell back to civilization." Without a single objection or comment from anyone in the group, the guys headed back to the resort, ready to put the whole ordeal behind them.

Chapter Three

JOSIE STRETCHED OUT IN HER chair and flexed her feet. Her eyes were closed, and her lips were upturned in a satisfied smile. Soft music filtered through the speakers of the spa, and the fluffy robe wrapped around her body felt as though it was made from clouds.

"Where are our moms?" Chloe asked, her voice barely above a whisper.

Josie shrugged. "If we're lucky, my mom is removing that stick your mom has lodged up her ass."

Madison scrunched up her face. "And setting fire to that outfit she showed up in." The girls all laughed in agreement.

"So, what do you think the guys are up to?" Lori asked.

Josie tried not to shudder as she thought about the possible hell her father and brother were subjecting Anders to. "I'd rather not think about that. Right now, I want to relax and enjoy some serious-business pampering."

"Thank you for inviting me," Lori said, the sincerity in her voice causing Josie to lift her head and face Lori.

"I couldn't imagine not having you here." Lori had interned for Josie during the beginning of her relationship with Anders and the aftermath that followed. Through it all, Lori had stayed by Josie's side, even when Josie had been turned into a villain by the media. When the opportunity presented itself for Lori to become more of a permanent fixture on Josie's team, Josie didn't hesitate to bring her on board.

"It's an added bonus that you don't take shit from Anders," Madison piped in with a chuckle.

"I wish we could say the same thing for Owen," Josie mumbled. Lori groaned when everyone turned their full attention to her.

"Please tell me she doesn't have a thing for Owen," Chloe said, shaking her head.

Josie widened her eyes and pointed at Chloe. "See? Even Chloe's got his number, and she hasn't known him nearly as long as you have."

"I've only met him like five times, and I wouldn't go there. And my standards are pretty low these days," Inky added, her expression colored in shame.

Josie's curiosity perked up at Inky's comment, as did everyone else's. "Care to explain?"

Inky fell back into her chair and closed her eyes. "I do not."

The other girls exchanged glances but decided to let things go for now. There would be copious amounts of alcohol over the course of the next few days that would surely loosen Inky's lips. For the next couple of hours, the girls sipped champagne while they had manicures, pedicures, and massages. It was the perfect way to start what would eventually become a very hectic but amazing weekend.

Once they arrived back at the resort, Josie, Chloe, Madison, Inky, and Lori decided to move on from champagne to rum punch, or just rum, from the taste of it, while Elizabeth went to her room to rest. Josie's and Chloe's moms had yet to return, although Josie's mom did send a picture of a rum bottle with a winky face emoji, so she assumed they were fine.

After their third round, Josie looked at her watch and blinked in confusion. "Shouldn't the guys be back by now? Has anyone heard from them?" Chloe and Madison pulled out their phones before shaking their heads.

Just as Josie started to call Anders, Inky gasped. Everyone looked in her direction, but she wasn't looking at them. Her eyes were solely focused on her phone.

"Holy shit!" She giggled, turning her phone around. There was a collective gasp from the girls, their expressions ranging from shock to amusement to concern.

"Is that Owen?" Lori whispered.

"Yeah," Josie answered.

"He's naked, right? I'm not seeing things?" Madison asked, her hand cupped over her mouth.

"Nope," Inky choked. "He's naked as a jaybird."

Chloe opened and closed her mouth. "But why?"

Inky turned the phone back around and shrugged. "I haven't the slightest idea, but I'll be damned if I'm not going to find out." A moment later, her phone dinged with another alert. When she saw the picture, she doubled over in laughter as Chloe pulled the phone from her hand.

Chloe narrowed her eyes and leaned closer. "What the hell is Walker doing?"

Josie mimicked Chloe's posture and shook her head. "Is he choking the...air?"

"What the hell happened out there today?" Madison whispered as Josie's phone vibrated beside her. Looking at the screen, Josie's confusion increased.

"It's from Anders. He and the guys just got back. He's going to shower and lie down."

"That's weird. What's the time stamp on those pictures?" Madison asked.

Chloe fumbled with the phone. "These are from, like, three hours ago. I guess they didn't have service until they got back to the resort."

Suddenly, a flurry of alerts flooded Inky's phone. With each picture, the girls became more confused, even as their sides began to ache from laughter. Images of Anders and Reid huddled together in what appeared to be a cave, Owen crouched naked in the corner covered in something they couldn't distinguish, and Walker swinging at a rock while Holden held him back came in rapid succession.

It wasn't until the last picture came through that the laughter stopped and shock strangled the air. "Inky, who sent you these pictures?" Chloe asked, gripping the phone tighter when Inky tried to pry it free.

"Greer sent them. Why? What did he send?"

"His dick," Lori murmured, her eyes still fixed on the image. "A picture of his gigantic, pierced dick."

Inky rolled her eyes, but Josie didn't miss the way her skin flushed. "So what? It's Greer. None of you can really be surprised after all the other pictures he sent. Clearly, they got into something."

Chloe shook her head and handed the phone back to Inky. "It's not the picture we're surprised by. Although I gotta say, I'm more than a little traumatized that I know what Greer's dick looks like."

"And that it's pierced," Josie added.

Chloe groaned. "Can we not talk about his dick and focus on what he wrote instead?"

Josie cleared her throat and spoke in a deep voice, attempting to mimic Greer's. "Don't tell me you don't want this again."

"Holy shit!" Madison said, her eyes wide. "Is this the low standards you spoke of earlier?"

"I fucking hate all of you," Inky muttered, slamming back her rum. "I'm going to need to be a lot drunker for this story."

Grabbing a bottle of rum, Josie and the rest of the girls moved to a couple of couches in the back of the lounge area. With eager expressions and cups filled with alcohol, they listened to Inky's story.

"We'd just gotten back from a show. It was that new band I'm digging right now, The Nuns?" she asked, looking at Chloe, who nodded. Inky pursed her lips. "If you would have just come with me, none of this would have happened. I totally blame you, just so we're clear."

Chloe covered her mouth, her eyes wide. "That was only a few weeks ago! Also, there was a screening of *Star Wars* that night. You knew better than to ask."

"Whatever. It's easier to blame you. Anyway, Greer volunteered to go."

"Wait a second," Madison interrupted, leaning forward. "How did he know you were going in the first place?"

Inky shifted in her seat. "We talk. It's whatever." Madison opened her mouth to speak, but Inky lifted her hand to silence her. "If you want to hear this story, you will stop asking me a million questions. The longer it takes, the more my buzz wears off." Josie leaned forward and refilled Inky's glass, a sly smirk on her face.

Inky looked at Chloe. "I was so much better off before you came along and introduced me to your friends. I could keep my shame and embarrassment all to myself."

Chloe winked. "Love me, you do. Now, on with the shame story, woman!"

"Anyway," Inky said, her voice full of annoyance. "We went to the show and it was amazing and Greer was really into the music and I don't know, it was hot. As soon as the thought crossed my mind, I freaked out and downed my drink. Then I downed another. I thought that eventually it would erase the image I had of him naked, but all it did was make it worse. Because he's a fucking groupie bloodhound, he knew exactly what I was thinking. It was like he could sense it. A fucking Jedi pussy-master or some other ridiculous thing you would call it."

Chloe burst into laughter, and everyone else followed suit. Well, everyone except Inky; she was pouring another drink. Once the laughter died down and the girls composed themselves, Inky continued.

"It was so weird," she whispered, almost like she was talking to herself. "He's always hit on me. Hell, I'm pretty sure he's hit on every one of you at some point, but this time, it was different. He was still Greer, cocky as fuck—I don't know, maybe it was the booze. Maybe it was the fact that I hadn't been laid in months. Whatever it was, the next thing I knew, we were naked in his bed, and that big pierced dick of his was making me scream for Jesus." Inky shuddered and took a big swallow of her drink. "The next morning was awkward as fuck, and I got my shit and left before he woke up. I expected that to be the end of it, but he just wouldn't shut the fuck up about it. He keeps sending me dirty messages, and it's fucking ridiculous."

"Wow, that sounds super familiar," Madison said, winking at Josie.

"Shut up, Maddie," Josie snarked with a smile. As much as Josie would like to forget the crazy, messed-up way her relationship with Anders started, there was no denying the similarities. Maybe there was hope for Greer, after all.

"I see the look on your face, Josie," Inky said, pursing her lips. "It's never going to happen. One, because I'm still waiting to make sure he didn't give me VD, and two, because it's Greer and I'm not getting mixed up with someone as fucked up as him."

"Yes, because getting mixed up with seriously damaged guys always ends horribly," Chloe sassed, receiving a nod of agreement from Josie.

"Now that all of you know my dirty little secret, can we please focus on what prompted this conversation in the first place? What in the hell happened on that trip today?"

"Maybe we should split up. Interrogate the guys individually," Josie suggested as she finished off her cup of rum. The truth was, Josie was more than a little drunk, and knowing that Anders was naked in their villa was driving her insane.

"Ugh, you're totally thinking about having sex with Anders," Madison said, her nose wrinkled.

Josie shrugged, her face unapologetic. "Damn straight. I'm totally about to hit that."

Chloe laughed and stood, looping her arm through Josie's. "Come on. Let's go find the guys and see what we can get out of them."

Inky looked at Lori and shook her head. "We're not going anywhere near those idiots. Let those three do recon. We're going to flirt with the cabana boys."

With a laugh, the girls parted ways, Josie, Madison, and

Chloe heading toward their villas, and Lori and Inky to the pool. As soon as they were out of earshot, Chloe leaned closer to Madison and Josie.

"Twenty bucks she fucks Greer before we leave the island."

Josie shook her head. "Nah, she'll hold out a little longer than that if for no other reason than sheer stubbornness."

"Did you see his dick?" Madison whispered. "I'm with Chloe. They're totally going to bang before we leave." With a handshake and a promise to find out what happened at the cave, the girls went their separate ways.

Slipping inside their villa, Josie walked to the bed where Anders lay facedown, a towel wrapped around his waist and beads of water still glistening on his back. Using the tip of her finger, Josie swirled the drops of water over Anders's skin, the soft touch causing Anders to moan and shift to his side.

"Rough day?"

"You have no idea," Anders answered, his voice gruff.

Josie's lips turned up, her eyes dancing with mischief. "Who knew cuddling with Reid could be so exhausting."

Anders shot up in bed, his wide eyes slowly narrowing. "What are you talking about?"

Chapter Four

ANDERS DID HIS BEST TO play things cool, but the playful mischief on Josie's face made his mind race. No more than a half hour had passed since they made it back to the resort. He found it hard to believe someone had cracked already.

He followed Josie's movements as she slid down the bed and dragged the tip of her finger up the length of his thigh. Her smirk was firmly in place, and as much as Anders wanted to yank her onto the bed and wipe it off her face, preferably with his tongue, he wanted to know what she'd heard more.

Grabbing her hand, he pulled her closer, making sure to skim her palm over his growing erection. There was no reason she shouldn't be as uncomfortable as him. When she narrowed her eyes, he smiled. For the moment, things felt even.

"Do you want to explain why you think I've been cuddling with Reid, or would you rather climb on top of me and let me show you why that's the most ridiculous thing you've ever said?"

Josie hummed and threw her leg over his waist, straddling his hips. "I'd say that pictures don't lie, but we both know that's not true. So why don't you just tell me about what happened today."

Anders gripped her hips and rocked against her, his eyes rolling back. "Today was total bullshit. Who the fuck thinks it's a good idea to ride through the jungle on four-wheelers then swim in some cave where people were slaughtered? You've got a fucked-up family, Ivy."

Josie let out a short laugh. "Don't try to confuse me. We're talking about you and Reid. Cuddling. We'll talk about my family's issues later."

"Why exactly do you think Reid and I were cuddling?"

Josie shrugged. "Because I saw pictures of exactly that. Not to mention Walker having a WWE match with the air, Owen naked in the corner in full-on Blair Witch meltdown mode, and of course, Greer's pierced dick. You boys had quite the outing—or inning, depending on how things went after the pictures stopped."

Anders sat up, his jaw set and his eyes hard. "What the fuck do you mean you saw Greer's dick?" Anders was two seconds away from completely losing his shit. Josie smirked again.

"Because, apparently, Greer and Inky had a drunken one-night stand, and his way of asking for a repeat was sending her pictures of his dick."

Anders blinked. That wasn't at all what he expected. "I'm not sure if I should still be pissed that you saw a picture of Greer's dick, or ask you to explain what the fuck you're talking about. Is this what it feels like to be a chick? Because if so, fuck this."

Josie laughed. "This is exactly what it feels like. So, Andersella, what would you like to gossip about first?"

Anders narrowed his eyes. "First, don't ever fucking call me that again. That was fucking awful, Ivy. What the fuck? Second, I need you to explain how you know about today so we can move on and get to the part where we take care of this." Anders lifted his hips, grinding his erection against Josie so she understood exactly what he was referring to.

Josie let out a low moan, and her head fell back. Leaning forward, Anders placed soft kisses against her exposed neck before biting down on her salty skin. She shuddered and her muscles tensed. For a moment, Anders couldn't remember what they'd been talking about or why it fucking mattered in the first place.

"I already told you," she exhaled. "Greer sent Inky pictures."

Anders groaned and dropped his head against her shoulder. Now he remembered. "Why did we invite him again? Because right now, I can't think of a single fucking reason."

Josie let out a low, throaty laugh as she wound her fingers through Anders's hair and tilted his head back until they were at eye level. "Because you spend just as much time with him as you do the rest of the guys, and it would have been super awkward to leave him at home?"

Anders shook his head. "Why couldn't his sister have gone into labor instead of Drew's?"

"Greer doesn't have a sister," Josie pointed out with a grin. "Now, are you going to tell me about those pictures, or am I going to have to describe, in detail, Greer's secret piercing?"

Anders's jaw snapped shut, and his blue eyes blazed with anger and jealousy. "I'm going to kill that fucker."

Josie rolled her eyes and leaned forward, her lips brushing against Anders's ear as she spoke. "He's got nothing on you."

"Don't be cute," Anders snapped. "You've seen one of my friend's dicks. That's not fucking okay."

"Well, if you want to be technical, I've seen two. Don't forget about Owen's sex tape floating around the internet."

"Jesus fucking Christ," Anders muttered, wanting to talk about anything other than all of his friend's dicks Josie had seen. "Shrooms."

Josie lifted her brows in surprise. "Come again?"

A devious smile stretched across Anders's face. "Again? I haven't even gotten started yet."

"You're only making this harder on yourself," Josie sang, her eyes dropping to where their bodies met. "The sooner you tell me what happened, the sooner we can get to that whole coming thing."

"Fine," Anders exhaled, rolling out from under Josie. "Owen, Walker, and Greer were flirting with some local girls, and their guys didn't like it. The boyfriends thought it would be hilarious to add a little bit of shroom juice to our punch. It wasn't a lot, or so I'm told, but by the time we'd reached the cave, everyone had gone batshit crazy. Well, everyone except Holden, Nathan, and your dad. They were spared."

Josie covered her mouth with her hand, her eyes wide. "That's fucked up! What if something would have happened to one of you? And Reid and Walker are in recovery!"

"Walker is never in recovery. But you're right, it is fucked up, but it's over now. No one was supposed to know about it, but thanks to Mr. Dick Selfie, I'm sure everyone will know before we sit down for dinner."

Josie scooted against his side and rubbed her hand over his chest. "I'm sorry that happened. I won't lie, the pictures are freaking hilarious, but that was a shitty thing of those guys and Mr. Dick Selfie to do."

Anders narrowed his eyes when Josie attempted to cough to hide her laugh. "I've about had it with you talking about dicks."

Josie lifted her brow, her eyes following the path of her fingers as she loosened the towel from around his waist. "You could always shut me up..."

Before Josie finished her sentence, Anders grabbed her

by the hips and rolled on top of her. Not giving her a chance to speak, he covered her mouth with his own. With panting kisses, he pulled her shirt over her head and made quick work of removing her bra. Once her chest was bare, he moved his mouth from her lips to her jaw and down her neck to her tits. "Don't even think about it," Anders warned, dragging his tongue across her hardened nipple as she opened her mouth to say something that, no doubt, would completely ruin the mood.

With a wicked grin, he curled his fingers around the top of her shorts and peeled them down her legs. Placing a soft kiss just below her belly button, he moved lower, smiling at the way her muscles clenched and her breaths left her lips in shuddering sighs. Nipping at her hip bone, he locked eyes with her once more before wrapping his hands around her thighs and anchoring her in place as he drove her to the brink of madness. Her pleas and struggle to break contact only spurred him on until her moans turned to cries of pleasure as her body jerked from the force of her orgasm. Then he did it once more for good measure, making sure the only dick on her mind was the one she would soon be riding.

Once her breathing evened out, Josie released a satisfied smile and tugged on Anders's hair until he crawled up beside her. With a lazy smile, she leaned forward and kissed his lips. "I'm so happy I get to have you for the rest of my life," she whispered.

Anders nodded and let his eyes drift shut. After allowing anger and bitterness to rule his heart for so long, he'd never imagined he'd be able to love someone as much as he loved Josie. She'd touched him at the center of his soul, and as terrifying as that was, he wouldn't trade that feeling for anything in the world.

"I'm going to need that in writing," he answered, his playful tone not revealing his swell of emotions.

Josie's eyes pinched at the corners as she smiled. "Never change, Anders."

Palming her ass, he squeezed as he shifted her body on top of his. Positioning her right where he wanted her, he smiled. "I couldn't if I wanted to."

The next morning, Josie, Madison, Chloe, Lori, and Inky lounged by the pool. Carafes of Bloody Marys, screwdrivers, mimosas, and every other drink considered appropriate for consumption before noon sat submerged in buckets of ice on a nearby table, along with an assortment of breakfast foods.

"I could stay here forever," Josie sighed, her face tipped toward the sun.

"Yeah, yeah, paradise, blah, blah, blah. I want to know what happened to the guys yesterday. What did you find out?" Lori asked, looking from Josie to Chloe.

"We should ask Inky," Madison chimed in, her expression full of mischief.

"Don't ask me shit," Inky said, her face bored, eyes flat.

"Oh, I don't know about that," Chloe giggled, her teeth trapping her lower lip. "Reid was pretty chatty after I worked him over for a bit. I'm sure Greer was more than happy to give you all the dirty details."

"Among other things," Josie muttered before coughing, "Pierced things."

Inky's face colored with annoyance when Josie and Chloe high-fived. "I didn't see Greer last night, so I don't know shit."

Josie smirked and took a sip of her mimosa before setting

her glass down and clearing her throat. "Here's the deal. The guys were drugged on shrooms yesterday. I won't lie, I'd be pissed off if everyone wasn't okay, but from what I understand, they're all fine. That means whatever stupid shit they did is fair game."

"Hear, hear," Madison cheered, her voice filled with laughter.

"That's fucked up," Inky said. "Mostly because it resulted in me being outed about Greer, but still."

Lori nodded. "I've never seen Owen so unattractive in my life. It was pretty tragic, to be honest."

Madison groaned. "We're going to have to stage an intervention before long. You know Owen far too well to still find him attractive."

"Shh," Lori hissed. "The guys are coming."

Reid was the first to join the group. "What's the plan with you girls tonight?" he asked, sitting on the end of Chloe's lounge chair.

Chloe set down her drink and scooted forward, wrapping her arms around Reid's waist. "We don't know. Josie's mom is in charge of tonight."

"Oh shit," Holden laughed, sitting beside Madison. "Whose idea was that?"

"Whose do you think? Hers, of course." Josie tried not to shudder. Her mother was a hot mess. Josie wouldn't be surprised to find male strippers and a tub of Jell-O on the agenda.

"I like your mom," Walker said, his lips morphing into a salacious smile.

Josie's face contorted with disgust as she stood from the lounge chair. "Did Anders tell you about all the guns my dad owns? I think it would be in your best interest to stick your dick in an electrified chain link fence before thinking about flirting with my mom."

"I swear to God, if I hear you talking about one of my friend's dicks again, I'm going to lose my shit." Anders stepped behind Josie and wrapped his arms around her waist, glaring at the guys.

"All of you are ridiculous," Inky muttered, sipping her drink.

"Those are some pretty badass tats you have," Walker said, his eyes raking over Inky. "Maybe you can tell me about them later."

"You can't be serious," Inky deadpanned.

"What's going on?" Greer asked, a tightness to his voice that anyone with ears would have noticed. Josie pulled her lip between her teeth to keep from laughing. If this turned into a who has a bigger dick contest, Anders might murder someone.

"We're talking about how many strippers Josie's mom is going to rent tonight," Inky said, her voice monotone as she flipped through her *Rolling Stone* magazine.

Anders narrowed his eyes at Inky before turning back to Josie. "I don't know how I feel about this bachelorette party shit."

Josie laughed. "Is that so? Do you want me to call it off? I'd be more than happy to."

Anders sighed. "But if you cancel, that means your mom won't have anything to do. Nothing good ever happens when she has free time."

"Sure, it does. How do you think I got here?" Josie asked with a wink.

"No, Josie. Gross," Holden said, his eyes screwed shut. "All of us shouldn't have to suffer from you fucking with Anders."

"So, what are you guys going to do while the rest of us are

stuffing dollar bills in strippers' G-strings?" Chloe asked, her eyes bright. Josie shook her head. Anders was going to Hulk smash something.

"Well, since we didn't have the bonfire last night for reasons…" Holden cleared his throat and tried to keep his laughter in check. "I thought we could do that tonight while you girls are out. I heard Mom telling Dad something about breaking Abigail out of her shell. I'm terrified for us all."

Chloe rolled her eyes. "No one is breaking my mother out of her shell. That woman is stone-cold."

"Not with me."

Chloe smacked her hand against Reid's chest. "Hush. No one likes a bragger."

Inky let out a disbelieving laugh and looked around the group. "Chloe, this entire testosterone fest of man meat is nothing more than a bunch of egomaniacs. They're all braggers. And yet, here you all sit…"

"*We*," Josie corrected with a glint in her eye. "Here we all sit."

Inky groaned and dropped the magazine on her face. "Why am I even here? You guys are terrible friends."

"I feel like I'm missing something," Reid said with a smile. "And I'm completely okay with that. Who wants another drink?"

A chorus of "Me" rang out, everyone clearly wanting the conversation to end. Anders, along with the rest of the guys, headed toward the drink table, while the girls settled back into their lounge chairs.

When the guys were out of earshot, Chloe turned to Inky, a sly smile turning up her lips. "I have a feeling things are going to get very interesting over the next few days."

"Stop looking at me. Whatever reality show drama you're expecting just isn't going to happen. End of story."

"I don't know," Josie chimed in, following Chloe's lead. "Did y'all see the way Greer acted when Walker hit on Inky?"

Inky closed her magazine and sat up, her eyes narrowed as she looked from Madison to Josie before settling on Chloe. "There will be no drama. There is nothing going on between me and Greer. And as far as Walker goes, he's worse than Greer. I'm already traumatized by that encounter. No way am I lowering the bar even more. At this point, I'd have to bury it!"

"You didn't mind when Greer buried his bar in you," Madison quipped.

"What did I bury?" Greer asked, a confused smile on his lips as he handed Inky a fresh drink.

Josie choked, her hand flying to her mouth to keep from spitting out her own drink. The image of Greer's piercing caused her cheeks to burn. Anders really was going to commit murder if things kept going the way they were.

"Thanks." Inky snatched the drink from Greer's hand and downed it before passing the empty glass back to him, "Keep 'em coming. I have a feeling I'm going to need to be wasted to make it through the next three days."

"Ms. Bane?" someone called from behind the group. "A package arrived for you at the front desk. We had it delivered to your villa."

"Thank you." Josie smiled. She wasn't expecting any packages, but she was certain it was something for the wedding. Her wedding. She was going to marry Anders Ellis. She looked at him and smiled. They'd started off under the most impossible circumstances, and here they were, about to be married.

"Keep looking me like that, and we're going back to the villa to check out another package."

"Gross," Inky groaned. "It's bad enough with Reid and Chloe. Now you two? This is why I'm an alcoholic."

Greer reached out and grabbed Inky's hand, pulling her to her feet. "Come on, let's sober you up." Without giving Inky a chance to object, Greer swept her into his arms, her long red hair flying behind them as he raced to the pool and jumped in, submerging them in the cool water.

"What the fuck?" Inky spluttered, wiping water away from her face as the rest of the group laughed.

"She's totally gonna hit that," Chloe whispered.

Reid shook his head, a playful smile on his lips. "That's it. I'm going to have to stop you and Greer from hanging out. You sound more and more like him every day."

"Hi, everyone! Anders," Sonya added with a wink.

Josie looked up, her eyes widening. "Mom! What the hell are you wearing?"

Josie's mother looked down at her outfit and shrugged. "It's a bathing suit."

"That is not a bathing suit," Holden said, standing to wrap a towel around her shoulders. The skimpy black bikini left nothing to the imagination, and the see-through cover-up somehow made it seem even more indecent.

"Damn, dude," Owen said, clapping Anders on the shoulder. "You just got a preview of what Josie will look like in about twenty-five years. Congratulations, fucker."

"I'm going to break your arm if you don't take it off my shoulder right now. What the fuck is wrong with you?"

"Everyone here is certifiable," Inky snapped, yanking a towel off the back of the lounge chair. "Oh shit, Chloe."

"What?" Chloe didn't get another word out before her mother came into view. "Sonya, what have you done?"

"I told you guys I was going to get Abigail to cut loose. Apparently, it just took a bikini wax to match that sexy little number she's wearing. Well, that and a Valium. Tonight is going to be so much fun!"

"Holy shit," Owen said, looking from Chloe to her mom. "This shit is getting ridiculously unfair."

Reid narrowed his eyes. "Anders, how's that whole hitting Owen thing going?"

"This is too much," Holden whispered. "I can't ever unsee any of this."

"Mom," Chloe whispered, her face frozen in shock. Abigail was wearing a minuscule red bikini, almost identical to Sonya's black one. That, however, wasn't what Chloe was looking at. Underneath her see-through cover-up were the very distinct markings of a tattoo. "Is that a tattoo?"

"Oh shit," Holden said, moving next to Maddie.

Chloe set down her drink—or dropped it, however you wanted to look at it—and moved closer. Josie stepped up beside her, unable to close her mouth. Abigail was the most uppity, proper person she'd ever met. She hounded Chloe constantly about her tattoos. There was no way it was real. It couldn't be.

"Mom, please tell me you didn't have anything to do with this," Josie said, her eyes darting from Chloe to Abigail. Chloe reached for her mother's cover-up and pulled it open.

"Oh my God. It's real."

"What is it?" Josie asked, moving closer. When she saw it, she gasped.

"Look, most of us aren't comfortable getting any closer than we are now, so if one of you could please tell us what it is, that'd be great," Holden said, keeping his eyes anywhere except on his mom's and Chloe's mom's half-naked bodies.

"It's a purple violin with my name under it," Chloe answered, her words choked. "Mom, when did you do this?"

"Last night," Sonya answered. "We might have had a little more to drink than we should have, and we wandered into a tattoo shop."

Josie spun around to face her mother. "Did *you* get a tattoo?"

The smile that spread across Sonya's face made Josie's skin heat. "Not anywhere that I can show you."

"Fuck this," Holden said, grabbing a bottle of vodka off the table and tipping it back. "I need this entire conversation never to have happened."

"Sucks, doesn't it?" Anders cut in, his expression smug.

"Karama really is a bitch," Holden conceded.

"So where is it?" Inky asked, clearly enjoying the opportunity of not being the one having her balls busted, so to speak.

Josie shook her head. "Oh no. We're not doing this. It's my wedding, and I get veto power over traumatizing conversation."

Inky shrugged, a mischievous smile on her lips. "That's cool. I have no doubt this is just the tip of the iceberg. I can wait."

Josie scrubbed her hand over her face and moved next to Chloe, who was still quiet. "You okay?"

"I can't believe my mom got a tattoo. I can't believe my mom got a tattoo of my name and a violin. I also can't believe she hasn't done anything but grin since she walked out here." Chloe snapped her fingers in front of her mother's face. "Mom! What's wrong with you?"

Abigail blinked and seemed to come out of whatever daze she'd been in. She looked from Chloe to Josie before leaning in. "Valium is awesome."

"Okay," Sonya laughed, swooping in next to Abigail. "We're going to eat a little breakfast before we hit the beach. You kids have fun. We'll be back later."

Before anyone could protest, the two women disappeared around the corner, leaving the group stunned into silence. Madison was the first to speak.

"My liver is going to take a beating this weekend from all the alcohol I'm going to need to black out everything that's happened so far."

"Ain't that the fucking truth," Anders said, downing the rest of his drink.

"Your mom is out of control," Chloe whispered, falling onto her lounge chair.

Josie gave her a wide, over-the-top, fake smile. "And she's in charge of our plans tonight. Isn't that awesome?"

"We're going to drink so much booze," Madison laughed.

"Say what y'all want. This is going to be a fucking riot," Inky said, settling back in her chair and slipping her shades onto her face.

"Your mom is single, right?" Walker asked, his cheek dimpled from his wide smile.

"Don't make me kill you," Chloe said, her voice completely serious.

Reid and Anders laughed and pulled Walker back from Chloe's death glare. "I didn't think it was possible for you to be any more of an idiot," Anders said. "Clearly, I was mistaken."

Maddie looked at Chloe and Josie before bumping her fist against her chest. "Shoulders, shovels, and alibis."

Josie let out a loud laugh, remembering the time Madison had said those exact words to her when Josie had debated if she could get away with burying Anders's body in the desert. It was a story Chloe was familiar with, and after a beat, she joined Josie's laughter.

"Any idea what the fuck they're talking about?" Greer asked, moving next to Anders and Reid.

"Nope," Reid answered. "But if it involves shovels and alibis, I'm pretty certain we don't want to know."

"Doesn't Chloe watch all those crimes of passion shows?" Greer asked, his brow raised.

"We all do," Inky said with a sweet smile. "You boys should remember that."

"I'm too pretty to die," Owen said, his eyes sweeping over the group. Josie didn't miss the way his eyes lingered a second longer on Lori, or how Lori dropped her eyes immediately, her cheeks pink.

Josie cleared her throat, causing Lori to snap her eyes in Josie's direction. Josie gave her a "Don't think I don't see that blush on your cheeks" look before turning toward Anders. "Do you know where my dad and Nathan are?"

"Yeah. They went to get some things for the bonfire tonight. I don't know what you need to get that would require them to go this early. It's wood. I'm pretty sure they're up to no-good, but after yesterday, I just can't be bothered to ask."

"Oh?" Maddie asked. "What happened yesterday?" She cut her eyes to Owen, who looked around the group, his eyes wide.

"Nothing happened yesterday," he said, his voice bordering on panicked. "Not a motherfucking thing happened yesterday." His eyes flew to Lori, and before anyone could say anything else, he reached for her hand and hauled her to her feet. "Come for a swim with me," was all he said before hauling ass to the beach, Lori stumbling behind him. Everyone laughed at Owen's quick escape. Well, everyone who hadn't been drugged laughed.

Anders and Reid were staring daggers at Greer. He clearly didn't remember sending the pictures to Inky. Which was awesome. For Josie.

Josie stood and slipped her hand inside Anders's. "Let's go for a walk," she whispered, tugging him away from the group. He cast a final angry glance at Greer before following Josie to the beach. Josie was quiet for a second before looking toward the water and watching as Owen tossed Lori over his shoulder and carried her into the waves.

"He better not fuck with her," Josie said, knowing it was a pointless statement but feeling the need to say it anyway. Lori had developed a crush on Owen when they'd met at a barbecue Josie and Anders had thrown. Owen had flirted, and Lori was completely smitten. Then Josie ended up working on a film with Owen, and he somehow managed to have Lori at his beck and call. It was eerily similar to the situation Josie had found herself in with Anders. Except for the one-night stand, fighting, fake girlfriend, shady reporters, and loads of baggage. Totally the same.

"Lori can handle herself. She sure doesn't take any of my shit," Anders said, bringing Josie's hand to his mouth and placing a soft kiss below her engagement ring.

"She likes him. Owen will never settle down. I don't want to see her get hurt."

Anders pulled them to a stop and turned Josie so he could wrap his arms around her, a sardonic smile playing on his lips. "People used to say the same thing about me too, you know?"

Josie huffed. "That's different."

Anders nodded, his expression mocking. "You're right. Owen and I are nothing alike."

Josie groaned and dropped her head to his chest. "Listen,

not everyone gets their happily ever after. What happened to Chloe and me with you and Reid doesn't always turn out that way for everyone." That's like lightning striking in the same place ten times!"

Anders chuckled and pressed his lips to the top of Josie's head. "Do you want me to talk to him? I don't know if it will do a single bit of fucking good, and if he tells me to fuck off, I'm not going to press. But for you, I will at least attempt to keep things from turning into a complete clusterfuck."

"Aww," Josie said with a sigh, batting her lashes. "My knight in shining armor."

"Don't be a smartass, Ivy," Anders chided. "Guys don't have those touchy-feely conversations you women have. And don't think I don't have questions about shovels and alibis. Y'all can be scary as fuck when you want to be."

Josie laughed and rocked up on the balls of her feet to plant a kiss on Anders's lips. "And don't you forget it."

"Like you would ever let me." Anders looked around, his gaze focusing on a small inlet. "Let's go fuck in the ocean."

Josie turned her head, seeing the hidden cove Anders was staring at. Her pulse quickened when she realized all their friends had scattered. "Okay."

Anders's eyes widened. "Are you serious?"

When Josie nodded, her world flipped upside down as Anders tossed her over his shoulder and ran to the water. In the beautiful seclusion of a rocky oasis, they melted into each other, the rest of the world fading away.

Chapter Five

"YOU'RE KILLING ME," ANDERS GROANED, his eyes traveling over Josie's body. She smiled and did a small curtsy.

"It could have been worse," she teased. "Maddie tried to pick out my outfit, but I vetoed. You've been tortured enough the last couple of days."

"You're lucky I'm letting you leave here in that dress. I have a feeling I would have locked you in the bathroom if it was worse than the one you're wearing."

Josie looked down at her dress and rolled her eyes. Sure, it was short, but it wasn't tight. The bottom flared out, the fabric swaying when she moved. Of course, Anders hadn't seen the back, so there was still a possibility of her being locked in the bathroom. Not that she would mind; the different scenarios of what her mom had planned for the night were far more terrifying.

"Are you guys planning on going out anywhere or just hanging at the beach?" Josie asked, wanting to change the direction of her thoughts.

"I'm never going anywhere with those fuckers again." Anders narrowed his eyes, his lips pursed when Josie laughed.

"You can't stay mad forever. It's unhealthy." Josie turned when there was a knock at the door.

"Are you ready?" Maddie asked on the other side of the door.

Before Josie could respond, she felt Anders's arms wrap around her. "Where is the rest of your dress?" His voice was low and dark and pure sex.

"I have no idea what you mean." She tried to sound innocent. She failed.

Anders loosened his arms and moved away just enough to touch the bare skin right above her ass before trailing his finger up the length of her back to her neck. "You seem to be missing fabric in this general area."

"How strange."

"Stop fucking with me, Ivy."

Josie spun around and wrapped her arms around his neck. "I think we both know that's the last thing you'd ever want me to do."

"This is bullshit," Anders groaned, leaning forward and nipping Josie's shoulder. "You're going out dancing looking like sin and sex, and I'm stuck here on the beach with a bunch of assholes whose number one source of entertainment is pissing me off."

"Josie, let's go!" Maddie yelled, her annoyance clear. Josie pulled away from Anders and gave him a sympathetic shrug.

"I promise I'll make it up to you when we get back."

Anders let out a heavy sigh and followed Josie to the door. Maddie stood on the other side, her arms crossed over her chest and her brow lifted.

"I was beginning to wonder if I was going to have to break down the door."

Anders let out a low whistle, his gaze bouncing between

Josie and Maddie. "And I thought Josie's dress was bad. Did you club Holden over the head for him to let you leave?"

Maddie twirled in her dress, letting out a small giggle. Not that the twirl did any good; the dress never moved. It was like a second skin of green silk. "I tried to get Josie to wear it, but she had to be difficult. No sense in letting it sit in the closet gathering dust."

Anders's eyes widened. "That's the dress she wanted you to wear?"

"Yup," Josie laughed.

Anders looked at Josie's dress again before shaking his head. "You two need to leave now before I lock both of you in the bathroom."

"Yeah, good luck with that. You should see the rest of them. They're going to give every guy in the club a heart attack when they walk in," Holden said, stepping behind Maddie. Clearly, he wasn't any happier with the situation than Anders. Boys.

"I'm liking this idea less and less," Anders said, his face pinched. "Why don't we just come with you?"

"I'm down with dancing," Walker said before slowing to a stop as he looked between Maddie and Josie. "Holy shit, you two are going to cause every guy there to leave with boners and blue balls!"

"That's it," Anders cut in. "We're not going to start talking about dicks again. Y'all get out of here before I change my mind. And if any motherfucker tries to touch you, I've already promised Inky I'll bail her out of jail if she fucks them up."

Josie laughed. "You didn't!" Anders's blank stare told Josie that was exactly what he did. "You're hot when you're jealous."

"I'm hot all the time, Ivy. Don't try to change the subject."

Josie rolled her eyes and gave him a quick kiss before

looping her arm through Maddie's. Just before they rounded the corner, Maddie looked over her shoulder, a mischievous smile on her lips.

"Have fun tonight, but y'all behave. I don't want to see pictures of any more of your friend's dicks!"

"Goddamn it, Maddie," Anders yelled as the two girls ducked out of sight, both of them breathless with laughter.

"He makes it so easy," Maddie said, fanning her red face.

"Stop picking on him," Josie said, but her expression was filled with amusement. "You two are worse than Holden and me."

"Oh sweet Jesus," Madison gasped, her feet stopping abruptly.

"What…" The words died in Josie's throat as she followed Maddie's line of sight. "Chloe is going to kill my mom."

Maddie nodded, clearly still at a loss for words.

"What the fuck?" Chloe said as she moved behind Josie and Maddie, Inky and Lori beside her.

"Damn, Chloe, who knew your mom was such a fox?"

"Not now, Inky," Chloe groaned. "Josie, I think your mom has drugged my mother. That or she's possessed, because I don't even know who she is right now."

Josie couldn't have agreed more. Abigail stood next to the limo, chatting with whom Josie assumed was the driver. Her hair was piled on top of her head in an intentionally messy bun, leaving an unobstructed view of the plunging neckline of her dress. There was no way she had on a bra. Of that, Josie had no doubt. Her dress was short and red and one hundred percent not something Abigail would have been caught dead in before. Maybe Josie's mom really had drugged her.

"Are you girls ready to go?" Sonya called, sashaying around

the corner like she was on some kind of runway. Josie's eyes fell shut, and she dropped her chin to her chest. Her mother wore a dress almost identical to Abigail's except it was black.

"Does anybody else feel like they're witnessing Stella get her groove back in real time?" Maddie asked.

"I don't know if I can handle this. We're going to have to drink a whole lot of tequila," Josie said, grabbing Chloe's hand in solidarity.

"Do we even know where we're going?" Lori asked, looking nervous.

"I have no idea, but the sooner we get going, the sooner we can get to work on a bottle of tequila," Josie answered, moving to the limo. It was going to be a long night.

"Shot! Shot! Shot!"

Josie laughed and grabbed her shot of tequila, raising it over her head before pouring it down her throat. Bass thumped from the speakers, and colorful lights danced around the dark bar. Ice sculptures behind glass cases were positioned around the room, illuminated by blue lights. One of the back rooms was closed off from the open dance floor, its entirety made of ice. Josie had tried to go inside, but even with the gloves and jackets the bar provided, it was too much for her California constitution. Of course, after a few more shots of tequila, it might be necessary.

She cut her eyes to where Sonya and Abigail were on the dance floor, dancing and flirting with locals who looked younger than Josie. The moms were definitely in need of cooling off.

Maybe she'd drag them back there with her to chill, for obviously different reasons.

"If your mom gets on that pole, I'm totally going to take pictures. I feel like it's only fair to warn you now."

Josie looked over at Inky and giggled. "Oh man, I can see my dad's face now! He would die. I don't know what it is about this island, but it's made my mother and Abigail lose their minds."

"I, for one," Chloe hiccupped, "traumatized as I am, couldn't be happier that your mother pulled the stick out of my mother's ass."

"You say that now," Maddie said, her smile wide. "I'm calling it now. She hasn't even begun to start racking up your therapy bills."

"Hush it, Maddie. She's already got a tattoo, she's dressed like...well, I can't call my mom what she's dressed like. She's taken drugs, and she's drunk more this weekend than she probably has in her entire life. I think we've hit our wall." Chloe and Josie locked eyes, Josie's brow raised in that *You sure about that?* kind of way.

"Um, Chloe," Lori said, her voice hesitant.

Chloe looked at Lori and smiled. "What's up?"

Lori looked toward the dance floor and grimaced. "I'm not so sure about that wall."

Everyone followed Lori's gaze. There were gasps, laughs, and stunned silence from the girls. "Mom!" Chloe shrieked, jumping to her feet. "Get away from that pole!"

The girls burst into laughter as Chloe darted toward the stage, trying to stop her mother from taking a turn on the pole. Josie narrowed her eyes, her vision blurry as she tried to locate her own mother. She didn't trust Sonya to not be waiting on deck.

"Come on, let's dance!" Maddie grabbed Josie's hand and hauled her to her feet. The room tilted on its side before righting itself. Stupid room. Inky jumped up, hauling Lori with her as the foursome moved to the center of the room. It didn't take long for the guys in the room to form a circle around them. The girls didn't care. They were there to have a good time, and as long as someone didn't get handsy, they weren't bothered. Josie giggled and moved next to Inky.

"Did Anders really offer you bail money if you'd kick anyone's ass who messed with me?"

Inky covered her mouth, her eyes wide as she started laughing. "Holy shit, I forgot about that. Your future husband is psychotic, in an annoying and sweet way."

"Yeah," Josie laughed, suddenly wishing they'd invited the guys, after all. The music changed, and the DJ came over the speakers.

"All right, guys. Let's take it back in time. Who's ready for an all-out nineties assault?"

Everyone in the club screamed as the immediately recognizable intro to "Ice Ice Baby" started pumping into the room. The crowd began to move in sync, the familiar tune creating an electric feel throughout the club.

Chloe appeared behind Josie, a bottle of tequila in her hand. "I can't stop what fate has decided, so I'm about to get shit-faced. Who's with me?"

Josie looked at her, confused, before whipping her gaze to the stage where their mothers were…twerking? Holy shit. "Give me that," Josie demanded, taking a long pull and coughing from the burn in her throat.

"Pass that shit around!" Inky reached out, her body moving to the beat as she tipped her head back and let the golden liquid slide down her throat. Things began to blur after that. The girls danced until sweat beaded on their temples and slipped down their spines, and the guys became bolder. Which was a huge mistake, obviously.

Inky had just moved nearer to fend off a guy who had come dangerously close to grinding against Josie when a familiar pair of hands gripped Josie's hips and pulled her against his chest.

"You're going to get me arrested days before our wedding, Ivy."

Josie gasped and spun around, the room making a couple more loops before settling on Anders's handsome face. Even in the darkened room with the pulsing lights, he was fucking delicious. His white button-down was open and rolled up to his elbows, his gray Henley stretched tight across his chest, and his jeans fit oh so right. She pulled in a deep breath and let her eyes fall shut.

"Hey, baby," she breathed, not even a little bit bothered that he was in front of her. A moment of clarity hit her, and she blinked up at him. "How are you here?"

Anders lifted his brow and smirked. "Your mother texted me."

"No," Josie exhaled. "What did she say?"

"She told me the sharks were circling, and the water was cold. I had no idea what the fuck she was talking about, but then she sent me a picture of Abigail on the pole and told me the name of the place, and that was about all I could stand."

"Coming to the rescue again," Josie giggled, wrapping her arms around his neck.

"You mom is a maniac, you know that, right?"

Josie nodded before her eyes flew around the room. "Is my dad here?"

Anders chucked. "You bet your ass, he is. He's going to take Sonya and Abigail home."

"Has he been drinking? I swear to God, if he gets on that pole with her, I might never recover."

"Honestly, I think she sent him pictures none of us ever want to see. He was very anxious to get to her and not because he was mad. The entire way here, he kept asking if it was okay for them to leave right away. He seemed very...excited. Actually, I need to stop thinking about it before I'm as traumatized as Chloe."

"Are you sure you're ready to be a part of my family? They're kind of a train wreck."

"Fuck no," Anders laughed. "But it doesn't matter to me how much of a disaster your family is. If I have to take them to have you, then bring it on."

"You say the sweetest things," Josie said, her nails scraping against Anders's scalp.

He let out a soft groan and dropped his lips to her neck. "I'm a motherfucking romantic."

Josie let out a loud laugh and hugged him close. "Let's have a drink."

Anders took a seat at their corner booth, pulling Josie into his lap. Reid, Chloe, Holden, and Madison were already there and offered the bottle of tequila to the pair as soon as they joined the group.

"Where are Lori and Inky?" Josie asked, pouring a shot in the glass and handing it to Anders.

"In the middle of hell and deep shit," Maddie laughed, pointing at the dance floor.

Josie looked to where Maddie pointed and let out a low curse. "Oh shit. This is going to be interesting."

On the dance floor, Inky and Lori were dancing together, seemingly oblivious to Owen, Walker, and Greer dancing with a few girls close by. Owen moved toward Lori just as a local grabbed her hand and spun her around. Lori let out a peal of laughter and continued dancing, having no idea Owen had been right behind her.

A second later, Owen grabbed Inky's hand and twirled her around, his smile wide. Inky laughed, her defenses down from the alcohol coursing through her veins. She swayed her hips, while Greer stared daggers at Owen

"They're going to fight," Chloe said, her voice matter-of-fact. "Thank God you picked Holden and Reid to be in the wedding party. Otherwise, you would need some serious Photoshop."

"All of these assholes will be in the pictures. I don't want to deal with busted lips and black eyes. Someone needs to fix this." Josie eyed the guys, but none of them made a move. She took another shot from the bottle, forgoing the glass and jumped to her feet. "Fine. I'll take care of it myself."

"Oh shit," Maddie snickered, her eyes shifting to Anders. "This is going to be good."

Josie moved toward the circle of her friends and stepped in front of Greer before he could cut in between Inky and Owen. "Hey there," she said with a smile. "You're not going to make me dance by myself, are you?"

A flash of surprise crossed Greer's face, his eyes darting toward their group of friends at the table before letting out a small laugh. "Keep your distance, woman," he joked, moving with Josie on the floor. "I have no interest in Anders trying to kick my ass."

"And I have no interest in you trying to kick Owen's ass two nights before my wedding," Josie said with a knowing smile. Again, a look of surprise flashed across Greer's face, but before he had a chance to respond, Chloe and Maddie joined the pair.

"For someone trying to keep the peace, you sure are playing with fire, dancing with a guy whose dick you saw twenty-four hours ago," Maddie said with a laugh.

"Maddie," Chloe squeezed her eyes shut like that would make the image of Greer's dick disappear. When she opened them slowly, she turned toward Josie, completely cutting Greer out of her line of sight. "Seriously, Josie," she said, looking toward their table. "I thought you were going to steal Inky from Owen, not get your groove on with Greer!"

Josie rolled her eyes. "I didn't really have a plan. I'm just kind of winging it here."

"Can we back the fuck up a second to the part where Josie saw my dick? Because I feel like I've missed something. Do I have a sex tape I don't know about?" Greer had completely stopped dancing, his eyes bouncing between the three girls.

"Jesus, I hope not," Maddie laughed. "Seeing Owen's was bad enough!"

"You watched my sex tape?" Owen asked, the sly smile on his face making him look like the cat who caught, then ate, the proverbial canary.

"Oh boy," Chloe said under her breath. "This is going to turn into a shitshow if Holden comes over here."

"Too late," Josie squeaked. "Abort! Abort!"

"Come on, boys," Inky said, grabbing Owen and Greer by their arms and pulling them away from the group as Holden, Anders, and Reid made their way back to the dance floor. "Let me show you guys the ice room. I think everyone could use a little cooling down." She looked at the group of girls and winked. "And no one needs to worry about anybody talking about their dicks in there."

With a giggle, she mouthed, "Shrinkage," as she hauled a very confused Greer and Owen to the ice room.

"What did I miss?" Lori asked.

"You don't even want to know," Chloe said, turning to Reid with a big smile. "Let's dance!"

"Come on, sweetheart," Walker said to Lori, seeming to appear out of nowhere. "You don't need to sit this one out."

"Thanks."

"Are you going to tell me what I missed?" Anders asked, wrapping his arms around Josie and swaying to the music.

"Oh, hell no. Some things are better left unsaid. Trust me."

Anders narrowed his eyes, and his mouth flattened into a straight line. "Y'all were talking about dicks again, weren't you? I swear to God, Ivy. You're going to make me kill someone on this island."

"Nonsense. You're too pretty for jail, remember?"

Anders let out a low laugh and shook his head. "You're going to be the death of me."

"Nope. You're stuck with me for a long, long time."

"Till death do us part," Anders whispered, his lips brushing against Josie's forehead.

Warmth spread through her body, a feeling of happiness that seemed to get stronger every day. "Not even then."

Josie swayed to the music, wrapped in Anders's arms, her eyes closed as the world drifted away. That was until she heard a loud roar of cheers from the front of the dance floor. They turned toward the sound, and both gasped in horror. On the stage, on the stripper pole, was Abigail.

"I thought they left!" Josie's eyes flew around the room, trying to find her parents. "Where are they?"

"Do you think they left her?"

"No way. Dad wouldn't have left her. Where can they be?"

"Maybe…" The words died in Anders's throat as he looked to his left. "Oh shit," he laughed. "No fucking way."

Josie looked to where Anders was staring, and all the blood in her body rushed to her face. "They didn't."

Anders was holding his side, and Josie wasn't certain he was breathing. "Well, I know where you got your love for wall sex from. Or maybe it was stall sex."

"Stop, stop, stop!" Josie begged, trying to get the image of her parents having sex in a bathroom at a nightclub out of her head. "This is too much. I don't even know how to categorize this level of trauma."

"My mom is on a fucking stripper pole, and I can see her G-string. Don't talk to me about trauma," Chloe said, her expression mirroring Josie's. "What the fuck is going on?"

"Go get her," Josie said, looking from Anders to Reid like they were crazy. "It's time for the parents to get out of here. Chloe and I need to get shitty."

Josie heard her mom let out a loud whistle and scream in encouragement at Abigail. "Anders is right. My parents are fucking insane." Grabbing Chloe by the arm, Josie hauled her toward her parents.

"Dad, you were supposed to take Mom and Abigail back to the resort."

"I am. Your mom and I just—"

Josie held up her hand. "I don't even want to know. But Abigail is on the pole. That's enough excitement for one night."

Everyone looked toward the stage just in time to see

Abigail grab Anders by the head and shove his face between her breasts and shimmy. "This is my hell," Chloe exhaled. "I'm actually dead, and none of this is real."

Josie grimaced. "It could be worse. She could have done that to Reid."

"Oh God. Thanks a lot, Josie. Keith, I think it's time for my mom to go back to the resort."

Keith nodded, seeming a little ashamed that he'd left her on her own while he and Sonya disappeared into the bathroom to do God knows what. "Yeah. I think you're right. You kids have fun."

Keith moved through the crowd, and after a bit of back-and-forth, finally convinced Sonya and Abigail it was time to go. Once they'd left, the group returned to the corner table, joining Lori, Inky, Walker, Greer, and Owen. Josie couldn't help but laugh at how Greer had positioned himself between Owen and Inky.

"I don't know about you," Josie said to Chloe as she passed her the bottle of tequila, "But I'm not stopping until I'm blackout drunk. I need to forget as much of tonight as possible."

"Give me that bottle," Holden said, taking it from Chloe and downing what looked like three shots. "I just saw my parents come out of the bathroom after having sex. Y'all don't have the market cornered on being traumatized."

"We're going to need a bigger bottle," Inky joked.

"And lots of them," Josie agreed.

Two bottles of tequila, a case of beers, and a whole lot of laughs later, they were all indeed, going to remember very little of the night.

Chapter Six

"IVY," ANDERS WHISPERED, PRESSING HIS lips to her shoulder. "Are you awake?" Josie groaned and threw her arm over her face, making Anders chuckle. "How's the head?"

Josie let out a muffled curse and grimaced. "Fucking tequila."

"I don't know why you do this to yourself. Tequila is no friend of yours." He'd stopped drinking well before the others, knowing there was a possibility he'd be carrying Josie back to the villa, which of course, he did.

"Jose is a jerk."

"Here," Anders murmured, handing her a glass of water and a couple of aspirin. Josie sat up, her face twisted in agony as she took the pills and downed the water.

"You're so good to me."

Anders chuckled again. "Don't give me too much credit. I'm going to extort sex from you later for making me go to bed with blue balls last night."

"What did I ever do to deserve such a gentleman?"

"You don't want a gentleman," Anders said, his voice rough and sexy. He trailed his finger under the bend of her knee and down the back of her thigh. Josie let out a soft sigh before dropping her chin to her chest and turning to Anders, a devilish smile playing at the corners of her mouth.

"You know, I've heard that having an orgasm can really help with a headache."

Anders returned her smile, already liking the direction of their conversation. "Is that so? And where did you hear this?"

Josie shrugged and reached for the hem of her shirt, tugging it over her head, leaving her in just her underwear. "I'm sure it was a man."

"Most definitely." Anders nodded, leaning forward and pressing his lips to hers. He moved one hand to her breast, letting the weight of it rest in his palm as he swept his thumb over her hardened nipple. He used his other hand to grip the edge of her underwear and slide them down her legs.

"I feel better already," she moaned, arching into his touch.

"You're so goddamn beautiful. I don't think I'm capable of being very gentle with you right now." He pulled her nipple into his mouth and bit down as Josie raked her hands through his hair.

Josie pushed on his shoulders, quickly rolling on top of him and causing a hiss to escape through his teeth. "Like you said, I don't want a gentleman. Not now anyway."

Anders gripped her sides and thrust his hips, his jaw clenching at the feel of her slick heat sliding against his naked flesh. Josie kept her eyes locked with his as she reached between them and positioned him where they both wanted him to be. Slowly, so fucking slowly that Anders thought he might lose his mind, she eased down on top of him until they were flush.

The veins in his neck strained as she began to move over him, her lower body lifting and dropping back down with each rock of her hips. His eyes wanted to roll back in his head, but his desire to watch her, feel her, breathe her was too strong. In a little over twenty-four hours, she would be his wife. His fucking wife. He still had no idea how someone who drove him absolutely insane had flipped his life on its ass.

He wanted to be closer. In a quick motion, he sat up, wrapping his arms around her back before flipping them, so his skin was all over hers. "I love you," he moaned as she wrapped her legs around his waist and lifted her hips.

"I love you too."

He reached between them, working her clit just how he knew she liked it. Her legs began to shake, and her body tensed as her head fell back and her mouth fell open in a silent cry of pleasure.

Anders let out a low groan, his body tensing as fire raced through his veins before exploding, stealing the breath from his lungs. He collapsed on top of Josie, panting and blinking away the spots in his vision. Beneath him, Josie leaned up and pressed a soft kiss to his jaw.

"Well, there goes my I-have-a-headache excuse right out the window," she said with a breathy laugh. Anders chuckled and gave her a quick kiss on the forehead before rolling off her.

"How about I clean up then go get you some greasy breakfast food."

"Okay, did you murder someone, and you need me to cover for you? Because you are really bringing your A game this morning."

"No murder." He smiled. "But tomorrow you're promising yourself to me for the rest of your life. If now isn't the time to be on my best behavior, I don't know when is."

"Anders," Josie chastised. "I call you Asshole as a term of

endearment. I know exactly who and what I'm getting. There's nothing I want more."

"Any hope I had that you weren't just as insane as your parents has now vanished. You must be crazy."

"Crazy in love with you," Josie teased.

"You just want my dick."

Josie shrugged. "There're perks to every relationship."

Anders laughed and patted Josie's ass before rolling out of bed and going into the bathroom. He took a minute to clean up before turning on the shower and walking back into the bedroom. "Go jump in the shower. You smell like sex and tequila."

He ducked and laughed when Josie threw a pillow at his head. "Your aim is shit. Go shower. I'll bring food back. And maybe even coffee if you're good."

Josie stood from the bed, blinking a couple of times to bring the room back into focus before brushing past Anders to the bathroom. "I'm always good," she called, stepping into the shower. Anders moved to the dresser and pulled out a pair of shorts and a T-shirt when his eyes landed on the box on top.

"Ivy," he called out. "What's in this box?"

"I have no idea! Just open it. I'm sure it's something to do with the wedding."

Anders grumbled under his breath before ripping the tape off the box and pulling out the object inside. All the breath left his lungs in a whoosh when he lifted out the heart-shaped silver jewelry box. His mother's jewelry box. He set it on top of the dresser like it was a bomb then pulled out the envelope. With shaking hands, he removed the folded piece of paper.

Josie,
It was so wonderful speaking with you. My heart is broken

knowing he won't allow us to be a part of such a special milestone in his life. Maybe once you two are married, you will have more influence in making him see reason. Until then, consider this your "something old." Don't worry, Anders will never know.

Tabitha

Anders crumpled the paper in his fist and dropped it next to the jewelry box. His pulse thundered in his ears, and his body shook with anger. Reaching for his phone, he dialed Nathan's number.

"Anders?"

"I need to talk to you now. Alone. Meet me in the bar." He hung up the phone, not bothering with niceties. He slipped on his shoes and moved to the door when he heard Josie's voice behind him.

"Everything okay? What was in the box?"

Anders let out a harsh laugh and shook his head as he opened the door. "I've got to deal with something. I'll be back, baby." He moved with purpose, no longer thinking about breakfast or coffee or anything other than talking to Nathan. He found a booth in the back and wasted no time ordering a drink. This was the last thing he wanted to deal with the day before he married the love of his life, and his rage was beginning to make his vision blur.

"Anders, what's wrong?" Nathan asked, his eyes wide at the sight of the man in front of him.

"My mother," he spat. "She knows where we are. She sent Josie a gift. The way the letter sounded, she made it seem like they had talked recently. But Josie hasn't said anything to me."

"Anders, you don't think Josie is going behind your back to try to help your parents get back into your life, do you?" The look of disbelief and, if Anders wasn't mistaken, hint of anger on Nathan's face caused Anders to shake his head with disgust.

"Of course not. I trust Josie completely. My mother is playing games. She said in one part of the note that Josie didn't need to tell me about the gift because I'd never know. It was a complete setup. My mother gave Josie the silver jewelry box I bought for her birthday when I was ten years old. It was from this old antique pawnshop, and all I had was the ten dollars I'd earned for taking out the neighbors' trash. The old lady who worked there was so impressed I was using my own money, she sold it to me even though I'm sure it cost a whole hell of a lot more. I'd know that thing anywhere. My mother wanted me to see it and hoped Josie would lie to me. What I want to know is why."

Nathan let out a heavy sigh and laced his fingers. "I fear I might be how your parents know where you are. They came by my office last week. They wanted to make sure I wasn't letting some woman take all your money, that your assets were protected."

"Are you fucking serious?" Anders hissed.

"I told them to leave or I would have security remove them. They refused to leave, so I stepped out to have my assistant call security. When they were finally escorted out and I was back at my desk, I realized I had the website for the resort open on my computer. I have no doubt they saw. Then when some of your wedding party was photographed at the airport, well, it wouldn't take much to guess the dates. I'm so sorry."

"But why? Why would they want to cause trouble with me and Josie?"

"Isn't it obvious? You're more vulnerable when you're alone.

With Josie, you don't need them. You have someone who won't let anyone take advantage of you. She's in the way."

"Do you think Josie talked with my parents and didn't tell me?" Anders whispered, feeling guilty for even asking.

Nathan shrugged. "Maybe. They might have ambushed her the same as they did me. I didn't tell you because you're about to get married, and the last thing I wanted you thinking about was your asshole parents. If they did it to her, I can see her having the same line of thinking."

Anders swallowed and nodded. He hated the thought of Josie keeping something from him, but from the way he reacted to the package, he could understand why. "I want to take out no-contact orders. I don't want them anywhere near Josie. Ever. She's too good to have to share the same air with them."

"I'll start the paperwork with the lawyer when we get back. Are you good?"

"Yeah, I'm good. I know I don't say it enough, but you're more of a father to me than my dad has ever been."

Nathan's face tightened, and Anders could see the color under his skin brighten before he let out a short laugh. "Josie has turned you into a complete softy."

"Is that your dad way of calling me a pussy?"

"Absolutely," Nathan laughed as he stood. Anders did the same, and before he knew what was happening, Nathan stepped forward and wrapped Anders in a tight hug. "I'm so proud of the man you've become. The old you would have immediately accused Josie of conspiring behind your back, but you didn't believe that for a second. I always knew you had it in you. You just needed the right woman to help you find it."

"Thanks," Anders said, his throat tight. "We're not perfect, but we're a team. I won't let my parents or anyone else come between us. Speaking of, I better get Josie's breakfast and coffee before she comes looking for me."

"Never did I think I'd see the day that a woman would have Anders Ellis whipped," Nathan chuckled.

Anders gave him a sly smile. "You know I'll get sex for this. And brownie points for when I act like an asshole. I'm not completely redeemed."

"Of course not. Go do what you need. I need to get back to Elizabeth."

"How's her sunburn?"

"Better. She's not asking that I just drown her in the bathtub anymore, so that's progress. How was last night?"

Anders let out a heavy breath and shook his head. "I'll tell you over a beer at the bonfire tonight. It's a doozy."

"I have no doubt. I'll see you later."

Chapter Seven

"WHAT THE FUCK?" JOSIE WHISPERED, her eyes wide as she looked from the note to the jewelry box. She thought about the way Anders had stormed out of the villa, and her stomach dropped. He couldn't possibly believe she would do anything to help his piece-of-shit parents, could he?

Josie sank onto the bed, her eyes scanning the room and landing on the white garment bag hanging from the closet door. The sight made her eyes sting and her throat tighten. The way he stormed out of the room, it reminded her of a time she would rather forget. A time when Anders trusted nothing and no one.

She stood from the bed, the jewelry box clutched in one hand and the note in the other. She paced around the room, her mind running one hundred miles an hour. A tear slipped down her cheek, and when she wiped it away, a trail of heat started at her feet and worked its way up her body. How dare he storm out on her the day before their wedding? How dare he think she would do something like this after everything they'd been through?

She had no idea how much time had passed before she'd filled her powder keg of anger. When the door opened, Josie spun around, her tear-stained cheeks flaming red. "Anders Ellis," she yelled, stomping to where he stood in the doorway, his eyes wide. "I swear to God, if you believe any of this bullshit…" She threw the crumpled piece of paper in his direction, where it hit his chest and fell harmlessly to the ground. "Well, I don't know what I'm going to do. But it's going to be bad, and you're going to regret it."

Anders set the small paper bag and Styrofoam cup on the table next to him then held up his arms in front of him. "Hang on, Ivy."

"Don't you Ivy me!" Josie felt a swell of emotions burst in her chest, and she wanted to hit something. She loved this beautiful, broken man so much, and if he crushed her heart with the next words out of his mouth, she wasn't sure she'd ever forgive him.

Anders let out a small laugh, which only seemed to make Josie angrier, before stepping forward and cupping her jaw. Without giving her a chance to pull away, he pressed his mouth hard and rough against hers. Josie froze for a second before pulling away, her anger fading to confusion.

"What do you think you're doing?"

Anders gave her a crooked smile, the one that melted and ignited her insides. "I'm kissing my fiancée. Is there a problem?"

Josie licked her lips and narrowed her eyes. "Have you been drinking? It's not even noon! What the hell is going on? One minute, you're all sweet and loving, then the next you're storming out of here like your ass is on fire, and I find this bullshit." Josie waved the jewelry box in the air and pointed at the note on the floor, her reaction bordering on manic. "And I thought…I thought…" Her voice broke and her shoulders dropped. She couldn't say it out loud; it hurt too much.

"Come here," Anders whispered, pulling her to the bed. "I'm sorry I stormed out like I did. When I saw the note and the

jewelry box, I lost it. And not at you," he added when she opened
her mouth. "I bought that jewelry box for my mother when I was
ten. She knew damn good and well I would recognize it immediately. She was trying to cause trouble."

Josie opened and closed her mouth a few times, trying to
process what Anders said. A thought hit her then. "What if it
hadn't been something you recognized? Would you have come
to the same conclusion?"

Anders dropped his eyes, letting the silence settle between
them. After a moment, he spoke. "Has my mother been in contact with you?"

'Yes," Josie answered without hesitation. "She sent flowers
to work to congratulate us on the upcoming wedding with her
number included on the card. I threw it in the trash. Then a few
days later, she called and pretended to be a supplier. As soon as
I answered, she started crying and begging me to convince you
to give them a chance. She said all they wanted was to be a part
of your life. I told her you were a grown man and I didn't make
decisions for you, that you would do what was right for you, and
I would support any decision you made. She said she understood
and hoped that in the future you would be as compassionate as
I was. I told her I'd prefer she not contact me again, and I ended
the conversation."

"Why didn't you tell me?"

Josie let out a sigh, the ringing in her ears slowly fading.
"Because you had just gotten back from filming, and I hadn't
seen you in weeks. The last thing I wanted to talk about was your
mother. Then we left for here a week later. I sure as hell didn't
want to bring her up here. Now, answer my question. What if
she had sent something you didn't recognize. Would you have
accused me of going behind your back?"

Anders scrubbed his hand down his face and let out a heavy sigh. "I have no doubt that I would have been angry, but I wouldn't have left. I would have asked you about it."

"Why did you leave this time? Where did you go?"

"Because I *knew* this wasn't anything you did. My mother was causing trouble, so I went to talk to Nathan. I told him I wanted no-contact orders against them so they couldn't bother you anymore. My parents are like a cancer, and you don't deserve to have them in your life. I hate that you didn't tell me about her contacting you, but I'm not mad. I understand why you didn't. I'm not perfect, Ivy, and I'm going to say and do dumb shit for the rest of our lives, but I trust you. Completely. You're the person I want to spend the rest of my life with."

Josie let out a soft cry and wiped under her eyes. "I'm too hungover for this shit."

Anders laughed and kissed her forehead before jumping from the bed and grabbing the bag and cup. "I got you a bacon, egg, and cheese sandwich, extra butter and bacon. And coffee, of course."

"I'm sorry for thinking the worst," Josie whispered, feeling ashamed. "I should trust you as much as I expect you to trust me."

"Don't worry about it, Ivy. We've got the rest of our lives to owe each other sexual favors."

Josie choked on her coffee, laughing. "Is that so?"

"You bet your ass."

"And who owes whom now?" Josie asked, the air around them becoming playful, comfortable, perfect.

"Well, it depends on where you want to start with the tally. If we go back to last night, I think I'm at least a blow job in the positive."

Josie took a bite of her sandwich, and her eyes rolled back. "Oh my God. This is amazing. This alone earns you a blow job."

"Ivy, you can't say shit like that to me." Anders reached down and adjusted himself, his erection straining against his shorts.

"And this coffee," Josie sighed, totally egging him on. "This might get you some of that wall sex you love so much."

"Woman," Anders growled, his face spreading into a wide smile as he leaned forward, ready to pounce.

"Don't you dare," Josie shrieked as she dashed around the bed and set down the coffee and sandwich. "I told you I'm too hungover for this!"

"We've already established what to do about that." Anders trapped her in his arms and pinned her to the bed before kissing her lips, jaw, chin, and nose.

"I love you," Josie sighed.

"I'm sorry we had a non-fight fight the day before our wedding. I didn't mean to upset you."

Josie raked her hands through his hair and smiled softly. "You did say we'd have a lot of make-up sex this weekend."

Anders grinned and placed his lips against her neck. "I did, didn't I?" Josie hummed as Anders moved his mouth to hers. "I love you too," he said before showing her just how much for the second time that morning.

Anders and Josie walked out of their villa toward the pool, the sound of cheering immediately greeting them as they came into view. Their friends lounged around the pool, their sunglasses snug on their faces and their drinks close by as they whistled, clapped, and catcalled.

"It's about time you two came out here," Maddie said, her smile wide.

"Probably because they came enough in their villa," Inky said under her breath. Everyone heard her, of course. Anders chuckled as he went to join the guys.

"Don't be jealous of my healthy sex life, Inky," Josie said, falling onto the lounge chair next to her and speaking low enough that the guys couldn't hear. "You have a perfectly willing pierced dick waiting for you to say the word."

"Also," Maddie added. "I have a vested interest in this. So, if you could just give it up, that would be great."

Josie let out a sharp laugh, her hand flying to cover her mouth, but it did nothing to muffle the sound. "Maddie."

"What? I'd rather she knows we're all betting on whether or not she and Greer have sex. Makes me feel like less of an asshole." Maddie said, making the girls laugh. Well, all except Inky. She was ready to throw the whole lot of them in the shrooms cave.

"So, are you ready for tomorrow?" Lori asked, changing the subject.

"Yeah," Josie whispered, leaning in closer to the girls. "Do you guys remember that package I got?" When the girls nodded, Josie continued. "It was from Anders's mom. She wrote a note trying to make it sound like she and I had been in contact and she believed I would help mend the relationship with Anders and his parents once we were married. She even sent this jewelry box Anders had given to his mom when he was a kid, telling me he'd never know it was from her."

"What the fuck?" Maddie spat, sitting up in her chair. "Is she out of her fucking mind?"

Josie shrugged. "I'm not ruling it out. Anyway, Anders got super pissed and I thought he was mad at me, but he'd gone to talk to Nathan about getting a no-contact order against his parents, so they couldn't bother me anymore. I feel so bad when I think about it now, because I automatically assumed he thought I was stabbing him in the back."

"Anders has a quick temper and a reflex to not trust," Chloe said gently, her smile reassuring. "It doesn't matter that you guys are about to get married. People are who they are. It doesn't mean he doesn't love you. I adore Reid, but he's got a lot of baggage. We all do."

"But Anders isn't that guy anymore," Maddie said, shocking everyone, including Josie. She shrugged and took a pull from her drink. "He's an asshole, but he would lie down and die for you, Josie. Even I can admit that."

"What did he do with the jewelry box?" Inky asked.

Josie bit her lip and cut her eyes to Anders. "He threw it in the trash. He said the woman he bought it for and the one he knew today weren't the same person. He said the woman she was today didn't deserve the love he gave to the woman she once was. It was kind of heartbreaking, to be honest."

"His parents are scum," Lori said, causing everyone in the group to look in her direction. "They're so much like Owen's."

Josie blinked and looked at the other girls, each of them wearing the same surprised, confused expression. "Is there something you're not telling us?"

Lori let out an uneasy laugh, her eyes darting to Owen before dropping to her lap. "He's not who you guys think he is. That's all."

Josie leaned forward and cupped Lori's hand in hers. "Don't let him get in your head. Owen is exactly who we think he is. He's complicated. Just like Anders, Reid, Walker, and Greer. But if you give him the chance, he will eat you alive."

"It worked out okay for you," Lori pointed out, her voice soft.

Josie let out a low laugh. "Yes, it did, but you remember what it was like. It's easy to forget all that now, sitting here on a beautiful island and preparing for my wedding. But my life was a nightmare. I wanted to give up so many times, but Anders was stubborn as hell. He nearly did to me what Owen might do to you."

Lori shuddered and looked at her hands. Josie knew the images going through her head. Images of Josie being mobbed by the paparazzi, nasty slurs all over the internet, and her picture splashed across the fronts of trash magazines over and over again. Even all these years later, people said awful things about her. People who had a hard time separating fiction from reality. Every time Anders did a movie alongside a female lead, internet trolls and crazy shippers would try to make photos of them seem like a new love interest. Josie would always be the bad guy in the eyes of the girls who wanted what she had.

"Just be careful," Josie added, patting Lori's hand.

"I can't believe all of you are drinking already," Abigail said, a huge pair of black sunglasses covering half her face. "We're going to have to look up a group rehab for all of you when we get back."

"Says the woman who's gotten a tattoo, pole danced, and shoved Anders's face in between her breasts," Chloe said, her brow raised in challenge.

"If you don't stop drinking, you don't have to deal with the hangover," Greer said, handing Abigail a Bloody Mary.

Abigail winced and mumbled under her breath something about killing Sonya. "If you can't beat 'em, join 'em." Abigail lifted her glass in the air toward Greer and took a tentative sip.

"Who are you?" Chloe asked, her eyes wide. "Clearly, you've been abducted by aliens and there is a pod person living inside you."

"The truth is, Sonya made me realize something. I have been alone for a long time, and as long as I am the way I am, that's never going to change. Seeing all of you happy and in love—" Abigail cut her eyes to Inky and Lori. "Well, most of you happy and in love, made me realize my life is passing me by. I have enough regrets." She looked at Chloe, her expression so full of remorse that it caused Josie's eyes to sting.

"Oh, Mom," Chloe said, her voice breaking. "I love you."

"I love you too. I'm so proud of you."

"That being said," Chloe added, pulling away. "Can you maybe dial back this new lease on life you've found until I've had a chance to adjust? Tattoos, I can handle, but seeing you pole dance and motorboat Anders Ellis was more than a little traumatizing."

Abigail, along with the rest of the girls, burst into laughter. "I'll do my best."

"That's all a girl can ask," Chloe said with a wide smile.

"So, what's on the agenda for the day, girls?" Greer asked, sitting on the foot of Inky's lounger and pulling her feet into his lap. She scowled, kicking his hand away when he rubbed his hand up her calf. He ignored her.

Josie shrugged. "I have to check on the flowers, food, and

a few other wedding things, but other than that, I just want to relax."

"How about we have that bonfire the guys still haven't had? Reid can bring his guitar and play a few of his new songs," Chloe suggested.

"That sounds nice, and something Elizabeth can do as well."

Everyone grimaced. Elizabeth had been holed up in her room with a severe sunburn since the second day they'd been there. Although, missing the shitshow at the club the night before might have been a blessing in disguise. Josie and Anders had forked over enough money; they didn't want to be responsible for therapy sessions too.

"Well," Abigail sighed as she stood. "I'm going to have a shot at the bar, then I'm going to find Sonya. If I can't sleep off my hangover, she doesn't get to either." The group said goodbye before circling up together, drinks in hand. That was when Josie realized Greer was still running his hand over Inky's leg, and she hadn't done anything to stop him. Josie smirked. Inky saw.

Jumping to her feet, Inky ripped her cover-up over her head, her wild red hair falling down her back and around her face. Her dark green bikini was nearly camouflaged by the endless colors of ink covering her skin. It was the first time she'd worn a bikini, and for a moment, everyone just gaped at her.

"Jesus," Maddie whispered. "Inky, that's hot as fuck."

Inky rolled her eyes. "Apparently, I'm willing to do just about anything to distract you assholes from your bet."

Josie snickered before clearing her throat and cutting her eyes at Greer, who had stilled completely, his brown eyes wide. "Yeah, I don't think that's going to go the way you'd hoped."

"Looking good, Inky," Owen said, tipping his beer to her

in appreciation while leering at the skin just above her bikini bottom. "What kind of hidden ink do you have under there?"

"All of you are pigs," Inky spat before pushing past Greer, who was now staring daggers at Owen. "I'm going for a swim."

"A swim sounds like a good idea," Walker commented, his eyes also following Inky. Greer muttered something about killing a motherfucker before Josie jumped to her feet.

"Okay, I have wedding stuff to do. As official members of my bridal party, you two have to come with me." Josie looked over at Lori and smiled. "See what you can do about keeping these clowns out of trouble."

Lori looked around with wide eyes. "Oh, you have got to be kidding."

"You've got this!"

As soon as the girls were out of earshot, Chloe spoke. "Josie, you're so going to lose this bet. No way they don't end up ripping each other's clothes off before this weekend is over."

"Anders said the same thing," Josie sighed. "He even bet me twenty bucks they'd bang. Now I'm gonna be out forty if I lose."

"Reid's with you, Josie. He doesn't think Greer has a shot in hell. I think he underestimates the effect Greer is having on Inky. I've never seen her so flustered."

"Also, Reid didn't see Greer's dick," Maddie said under her breath.

Chloe groaned. "I'd really like to forget I ever saw that. I'm way closer to him than you guys. I have to practically live with him on the tour bus. I just need that image vanquished from my memory."

Josie shook her head. "I know I put Lori in charge of holding down the fort, but I think that much testosterone might be too much for any one person to handle. So let's get this wedding stuff out of the way and get back to the group before all hell breaks loose."

"Let's," Chloe and Maddie agreed.

Chapter Eight

THE SMELL OF SALT, SAND, and smoke lingered on the breeze. Heat licked the air, the flames from the fire dancing and casting long shadows around the group. Anders settled back in his seat and pulled Josie down with him, hugging her close to his chest. He looked around the group, their friends and family, and felt a sense of peace wash over him. He didn't care that he didn't have any biological family to witness his wedding. The people around him, crazy though they might be, were all the family he needed.

"What are you thinking about so hard?" Josie asked, turning in his lap so she could wrap her arms around his neck and press her lips to his cheek.

"That I can't wait for all these fuckers to go back home. I don't want to see any of them for the rest of the year."

Josie threw her head back and laughed. "You're such an asshole. You're also full of shit."

Anders nodded. "I'm just happy, Ivy. I'm finally fucking happy, and it's all because of you."

"As much as I'd like to take the credit, none of this would have been possible if you hadn't been willing to try."

"You made it really fucking easy for me to make that decision…eventually," he added with a chuckle. "God, you were such a pain in my ass."

"Says the asshole," Josie said with a smile.

"It was worth it, though. I'd do it all over again if it meant that I got to have you."

"Fuck that. I would have gone home and masturbated and just imagined having wall sex with you." Josie's eyes sparkled with mischief as Anders pressed his lips into a thin line.

"I'm trying to be romantic and shit, and you're fucking it all up with that smart mouth of yours."

"Well, how about you shut me up?" she whispered, her lips stretched into a smile as she covered his mouth with hers.

"That's more like it," Anders grumbled, his hands finding her hair and deepening the kiss. In the dark, lulled by the sounds of the ocean and the crackling of the wood on the fire, it was easy to forget they weren't alone.

"I hope you know everyone is picturing you two having sex," Inky said, her voice breaking through the bubble they'd created around themselves.

"The hell, everyone is," Holden said, his expression full of horror.

"Yeah," Keith added, his voice flat as he took a sip of his beer. "That's going to be a no for me."

Sonya shook her head. "Of course, I'm not thinking about Josie having sex!"

"No one here missed that she said nothing about Anders, right?" Inky asked, the smile in her voice almost giddy.

"I swear to God, woman, if you don't stop hitting on Anders, I'm going to burn down your She-shed."

Sonya laughed and wrapped her hands around Keith's arm. "You know I only have eyes for you."

"Your parents are fucking insane, Ivy. Certifiable."

"You know, a part of me wants to defend them, but a bigger

84

part, the part that has been exposed to things I never ever want to think about again, has to agree with you."

"So, Reid, I hear you guys are getting close to putting out a new album," Nathan said, thankfully steering the conversation away from the gutter. With this group, they were always just one step away from crossing into uncomfortable territory. Like talking about his friends' dicks.

"Soon," Reid said, pulling Anders from his thoughts. "We've got a couple songs we want to mess with a bit, but it's looking good. Adding Chloe to the band permanently really has been a game changer."

"It sure has. Now every other song on the album won't make you want to slit your wrists," Greer said, dodging Reid's fist. "What? I'm just telling the truth! This album has been a lot of fun."

"You just like that you have solos and get to sing more," Chloe joked.

"Says the girl who has her own song," Greer shot back, smiling when she scowled.

"What?" Josie gasped as the rest of the group showed their surprise.

"Why didn't you tell me?" Abigail asked.

"Because I don't know if it will make the final cut," Chloe grumbled, throwing her beer cap at Greer's head. "Jerk."

Reid laughed and leaned forward, tugging her hand and pulling her from her chair into his lap. "It's going to make the cut. She's just nervous."

"Why don't you sing it now?" Josie suggested, her eyes falling to the guitar next to Reid's chair. Just as Chloe opened her mouth to speak, a line of tiki torches came into view.

"Oh!" Josie gasped. "It's time!"

"What's going on?" Keith asked, the rest of the group looking just as confused. Well, everyone except Chloe and Maddie.

"Well, while we were out doing wedding stuff earlier, we were discussing what to do tonight. Instead of us just sitting around and getting shit-faced, we thought it would be fun to play games while getting shit-faced. I mean, I'm not getting shit-faced," Josie said, pointing at herself before turning her attention to Anders. "And you're not getting shit-faced, but there's no reason we can't laugh at these idiots doing it."

"What have you done?" Anders chuckled, standing from his chair and helping Josie to her feet.

She smiled. "You'll see. I'll be right back."

Josie jogged over to one of the guys carrying a tiki torch and pointed to where she wanted him to set up. While Josie directed traffic, Anders opened another beer and moved next to Maddie. "She does realize getting these assholes drunk might lead to more trauma. Or a fight." Anders thought about the way Greer had acted when Owen was dancing with Inky the night before. A fight was definitely a possibility.

Maddie shrugged. "Maybe it will motivate people to up their game."

Anders was quiet for a minute before he grinned and turned to Maddie. "You're talking about the bet."

"I mean, I do have twenty bucks on the line. But Inky knows all about it, so I don't feel like a jerk. And if a little healthy competition pushes Greer to maybe be a little more honest with himself that Inky is more than just another booty call, well, then I don't see the harm."

Anders shook his head. "We never stood a chance against any of you."

"Not a single one," Maddie said with a laugh, surprising Anders when she reached over and gave him a hug. "I'm so glad we didn't have to bury you in the desert."

Anders patted Maddie on the back. "Well, that makes two of us."

"Not you too," Holden said with a dramatic sigh. "Having Josie and Mom fall all over this guy is bad enough."

"Oh, hell no," Anders said with a laugh. "She's all yours. I can barely handle the one I have. And we're not going to talk about your mother because that would just be uncomfortable for all of us."

"In-fucking-deed," Holden said, clinking his beer with Anders's.

"I see booze and food. I already like whatever it is Josie's set up," Walker said, moving toward the tables.

"Did she come up with all this on her own?" Holden asked.

"No. While we were finalizing wedding plans and chatting about tonight, one of the ladies in charge of the wedding mentioned they had these beach party packages they offered guests. They come out and set up drinks, food, music, and a few games. It sounded like a fun way to relax before Josie goes into full freak-out mode."

Anders turned to Maddie. "Freak-out mode? What the fuck does that mean?"

"Calm down, fool," Maddie said with an eye roll. "She has a lot to do tomorrow, and it's stressful and overwhelming. It's one of the main reasons Holden and I decided to elope. Fuck all that noise."

Anders pursed his lips, but he let it go. He knew women went a little crazy when it came to weddings, and even though

Josie had been pretty chill, she had her moments. "What are they setting up over there?"

"It looks like limbo. After a few drinks, people are going to bust their asses," Holden laughed.

"I think she got a cool light-up beach volleyball set and some other game I can't remember. It'll be fun. Come on, let's grab a drink!" Maddie led the group to where Walker, Owen, Keith, Nathan, and Greer already stood, drinks in hand.

Anders took a sip from his drink and looked around the beach. Tiki torches lined the perimeter, boxing them in around the already roaring bonfire. "Alcohol and fire. What could possibly go wrong?"

Josie stood with one arm behind her back, her feet spaced apart, and her eyes locked with Anders's. To her left, Inky, Chloe, and Lori stood in a similar position with Greer, Reid, and Owen across from them. Between each group was a long white table containing red plastic cups filled with beer.

"Anders, I don't think you boys know what you're getting yourself into," Maddie said, her voice playful.

Greer shook his head. "You girls always talk so much shit. I don't see you playing. Are you scared?"

A Cheshire cat smile spread across Maddie's face at the same time Holden groaned. "Dude, you just fucked all of us."

Maddie looked at Lori. "Why don't you and Owen take over for me and Holden to make sure no one cheats. Apparently, I need to back up my shit talk."

Lori grinned and nodded. "Come on, Owen. I have a feeling we're going to be glad we're not playing."

"Flip cup not your game?" he asked, the pair moving so Holden and Maddie could take their places.

"Not really. But I'm always willing to try something new."

Owen smirked. "Is that so?"

Even in the soft glow from the tiki torches against the night sky, Josie could see the bloom of color spread under Lori's skin.

"Are you guys ready to start?" Josie asked.

Holden let out another sigh and looked at Greer. "How much do you know about Josie and Maddie?"

Greer shrugged. "I don't know. They're friends. Related now. They're down with Chloe. They like to play with clothes. Oh, and they drink a shit-ton of tequila."

Inky rolled her eyes. "Sweet Jesus."

"And do you have any idea where they found their love for playing with clothes and drinking a shit-ton of tequila?" Holden asked, his line of questioning obvious.

Greer gave him a blank stare as Josie and Maddie giggled.

"College. They met in college, you idiot. Where they played this fucking game every damn weekend. Hell, I think they have a damn certificate for best flip cup team or some shit. We will not win this."

"You hustling me, Ivy?" Anders asked, his voice filled with mirth.

Josie bit her lip and shrugged. "Maybe."

"I see how it is."

"You don't get to be the best at everything."

"Before Anders and Josie take their conversation in

a direction I won't be able to forget, can we just get this ass-whooping started?"

Josie looked at Holden and laughed. "Sure, bro. Lori, count it down."

"One, two, three, *go!*"

Chloe and Reid were up first. They slammed their cups against the table before chugging the beer and placing the cup on the edge of the table. Chloe was the first to flip her cup, but it landed on its side. The music from the small DJ station the hotel provided kicked up the volume as the group yelled words of encouragement and a healthy dose of trash talk. It took Reid only two tries to flip his cup before Greer knocked back his drink. One more flip and Chloe landed it. Then Inky snatched up her cup and downed it in one go. She set the cup on the edge of the table and, in one smooth motion, flipped her cup.

Maddie let out a peal of laughter just as Greer landed his cup as well. Grabbing her cup, she let her head fall back and downed her beer in sync with Holden. In a move that surprised everyone, Holden landed his cup in one flip and Maddie missed.

"Shit," she murmured, her eyes darting to Anders as he downed his beer. On her second try, she landed the cup and turned to Josie. "Deep-throat that shit!"

Anders choked on his beer as Josie drank hers and set her cup on the edge. She looked at Anders who had also positioned his cup and smiled. Never taking her eyes off his, she flipped the cup, landing it perfectly before he could even touch the red plastic. All the girls let out screams as they high-fived each other.

"See," Holden said, unsurprised. "Even when they fuck up, you can't beat them."

Anders shook his head. "I want a rematch. Maddie, you

can't talk about my girl and deep-throating and expect me to concentrate."

Maddie laughed and nodded. "Fine. Let's rotate teams. Best out of five is the winner. And the winners get to pick one of the activities we have out here for the losers to do."

"I don't want in on this bet," Holden said. Clearly, he knew the odds were against him.

"Fuck that. We've got this," Walker said, stumbling from the drink table. "We used to play this shit in rehab all the time. I'm a flip cup master."

"I don't think that's how rehab is supposed to work," Inky commented, her words laced with confusion.

Walker winked. "Then you're not going to the right rehab."

Turned out, Walker really was good at flip cup. And surprisingly, so were Josie's parents. She didn't want to think about how they'd learned their skills. They'd met in college. The thought of her parents drunk at frat parties and making out in basements caused a shiver to run up her spine. Just no. In the end, her dad's skills and Lori's lack thereof didn't matter. Josie and Maddie together wouldn't be beat, and the girls won in three games.

"So, what should we have them do first?" Inky asked, her eyes dancing.

"Josie, what are our options?" Lori asked. Josie noticed the way Lori swayed and her smile was relaxed. It was the first time she'd really seen Lori drunk the whole weekend.

"Well, we have hula hoops, light-up volleyball, and those pugil jousting poles used to knock your opponent off small platforms."

"Oh my God, one hundred percent hula hoops. With Owen and Walker," Maddie laughed.

Owen smirked. "Clearly, you're doubting my skills, girl. You might know how to flip a cup, but moving my hips has never been an issue."

"Less talking, more making an ass out of yourself," Holden said, a slight tinge of annoyance to his voice. Josie wasn't surprised. She was more than certain both Holden and Anders had had enough talk about dicks and sex tapes and anything else to do with fucking from the other guys.

While Owen and Walker got into position, Abigail walked out to join them. "Let me show you boys how it's done."

"You mom is like the gift that keeps on giving," Inky said, bumping her shoulder to Chloe's.

Chloe disagreed. "She's hit her wall. We've already hit peak trauma. This is nothing. She's hula-hooping, not flipping upside down on a stripper pole."

"If you say so," Inky teased.

The music changed, the beat quick but sexy. Abigail spun the hoop around her waist and hit a rhythm right away. She laughed at Walker and Owen as they struggled to get their motion right. Owen was the first to find his groove, but as soon as he tried to smile smugly at the group, the plastic ring fell into the sand. Walker was hopeless. After his sixth try, he moved the hoop to his arm and spun it around while taking a sip from his beer.

"I don't need all that motion of the ocean bullshit. My boat is a fucking cruise liner."

Owen shook his head as everyone burst into laughter. "We're sending you back to rehab when we get home."

Walker grinned. "Fine by me. Apparently I need to brush up on my flip cup."

"This is it, Sonya," Keith said with a sigh. "These are the people we have to look forward to running the country."

"Let's be honest," Nathan said with a chuckle. "We aren't in danger of Walker running anything."

"Okay, who's up next?" Josie asked, already knowing what she wanted to see follow this.

"Depends on what you have in mind," Holden said, eyeing the hula hoops. Josie had seen her brother dance. He'd be worse than Walker.

"You and Dad on the platforms with the pugil jousting poles!"

Everyone cheered as Holden and Keith climbed onto the small wooden steps, and each took one of the long plastic poles with heavy padding on the ends. They looked like giant Q-tips. The rules were simple; the last one standing on their step was the winner.

"Go!" As soon as the words left Josie's mouth, her dad swung his pole forward and whacked Holden in the shoulder. Holden tipped on his side but quickly righted himself.

"I see how it is, old man," Holden said, his balance still a little wobbly.

Keith smiled. "You didn't think I was going to take it easy on you, did you?"

"Let's go, then." Holden swung high, and Josie's dad ducked. The momentum of Holden's swing almost threw him off the platform again. That was when Keith went for the kill. He swung low, hitting Holden in the hip, and a second later, Holden was flying through the air and landing with a thud in the sand.

"Hell yeah! You totally kicked his ass!"

"Mom," Josie said, her mouth hanging open. "You're trash-talking about your husband kicking your son's ass. Shouldn't there be at least a hint of conflict there, or no?"

Sonya shrugged. "Holden's grown. I can cheer for your old man to show you two who's boss every now and then. It's hot."

"Nope. Not doing this with you," Josie said, turning away from her mother. There was far too much talk about sex with these people. "Who's next?"

"Come on, Reid," Greer said, tossing him one of the poles. "Let's see what you got."

Reid laughed and stepped onto the platform across from Greer. "Don't get mad when I embarrass you."

Greer rolled his eyes and cracked his neck. "In your dreams."

Greer landed the first blow, but unlike Holden, Reid kept his balance and returned a hit just as hard. The group stood around cheering and taunting the guys as they literally beat the hell out of each other. Josie was glad the ends were super padded or else they'd likely be covered in bruises. Hell, she still wasn't one hundred percent sure they wouldn't be anyway. After a couple minutes of trash talk, a few of the onlookers wandered to the food table or the limbo pole.

Walker moved next to Inky and pointed at the limbo pole where Abigail was getting assistance from one of the resort employees as she struggled to bend her back to get under the pole. "What are you, five feet tall? I bet you're flexible enough to get under that with no problem."

Before Inky could open her mouth, Josie gasped and Anders let out a low whistle. Distracted by Walker's conversation with Inky, Greer didn't even see it coming until it was too late. Reid landed a solid hit to his shoulder, and in dramatic fashion, Greer flew through the air before landing in the sand, much like Holden had done, but far worse due to his distraction. Inky's eyes widened, and she rushed over to Greer's side, with Josie and the rest of the group following behind.

"Shit, Greer, are you okay?" Inky asked.

"Dude, what the fuck? You didn't even try to block that." Reid snapped his fingers in front of Greer's face when he suddenly pulled in a sharp breath.

"Holy shit," Greer coughed. His eyes found Inky's, and he must have noticed the panicked look on her face because his pained expression morphed into a cocky grin. "Were you worried about me, Inky?"

Inky pursed her lips and stepped over his legs, straddling his body. She leaned down over him and took his face in her hands. Josie lifted her brow, wondering if Inky was going to give in to Greer, after all. She should have known better.

"You," Inky said in a soft and sultry voice before her expression changed and everyone knew she was up to no-good. "Got knocked the fuck out!"

"Oh my God," Lori laughed. "You just went all Smokey on him! This is amazing!"

"Come on, Deebo," Inky joked, reaching for Greer's hand to help him up. But Greer had other plans. Instead, he wrapped his arms around Inky and pulled her onto the beach, rolling on top of her and pinning her arms above her head.

"Who's Deebo now?" he asked. Inky fought to get out from under him, but Josie had seen enough.

"I'll feel like I'm watching soft-core porn. Let's leave these two to whatever the hell it is they're doing," Josie said, turning away. She took a couple of steps before she spun around. "Walker!"

He let out a quiet chuckle and shrugged before following the rest of the group. Over the next couple of hours, people divided up, some playing volleyball, some working on their limbo skills, which had become dramatically worse as the night had worn on and the alcohol disappeared.

"They look cozy," Inky said, stepping next to Josie and nodding toward Abigail and the guy who'd helped her with the limbo stick earlier.

Josie smirked. "So did you and Greer. You gonna make me lose my money, Inky?"

"You realize you're a horrible person for making a bet like that, right?"

"Tell me right now that if the roles were reversed, you wouldn't have done the same thing, and I'll apologize."

Inky rolled her eyes. "Well, obviously, I would have done the same thing. You think the band didn't have a bet on when Chloe and Reid would bang? That doesn't mean I can't complain and whine about it now that the shoe's on my foot."

Josie laughed and wrapped her arm around Inky's shoulder. "I'm so happy I met you. You're good people."

"Don't suck up to me," Inky sassed before returning Josie's hug. "You're pretty fucking awesome yourself."

Maddie walked over to where they stood, her face apologetic. "Guys, I know we're having fun and all, but Josie, we have a lot going on tomorrow, so I think we should call it a night."

Josie gave Maddie a salute. "Go round up the girls. I need to tell Anders I'm leaving."

"Is he still pissed you're not staying in the villa with him tonight?" Inky asked.

Josie sighed. "For all the progress he's made, he's still Anders."

"So, that's a yes?" Inky laughed.

"That's a yes. I'll meet you guys there."

Josie moved over to where Anders stood next to Keith and Holden and grabbed his hand. "It's late. We're going to head to the bridal villa."

"Bridal villa," Anders said, his voice mocking. "This is bullshit. We're getting married tomorrow, and I have to sleep without you because of some old wives' tale?"

Josie grinned and laced her fingers together behind his neck. "One night won't kill you. We have the rest of our lives together," she whispered.

"You're damn right, we do." He wrapped his arms around her waist and pulled her close. "I love you, Ivy."

"I love you too."

"Let me walk you to the villa."

Josie smiled. "Okay." They turned and, hand in hand, made their way through their friends, telling them goodnight. They were just moving past where Greer and Walker were on the platforms beating the hell out of each other, when it happened. Greer landed a solid hit against Walker's chest that sent him flying backward toward Anders, who was standing right next to the bonfire. Anders let out a low curse before shoving Josie out of the way and bracing for the impact of Walker's body. They collided and stumbled back, Anders's body heading straight for the huge fire before Keith dove and sent both of them to the ground.

"Anders!" Josie screamed, falling next to him on the sand. "Are you okay?"

Anders coughed and sat up with Keith's help. "I'm okay. Shit, Keith, thank you. That idiot almost knocked me into the damn fire."

The three of them turned to where Walker lay facedown in the sand, his body shaking with laughter. "You guys are going to take care of that rehab thing when you get back home, yeah?" Keith asked.

Josie and Anders both let out a light laugh. "Yeah. But we have to find one that doesn't allow beer pong," Josie said, standing.

"Smart call. You kids get out of here. I'll make sure everything is taken care of. We'll see you two tomorrow."

"Thanks, Dad," Josie said, giving him a tight hug before turning and pulling Anders with her, away from the fire and to the safety of the villas.

"This has been a fucking crazy few days," Anders said, shaking his head.

"So crazy." They walked hand in hand until they reached the bridal villa, and Anders let out a long sigh.

"I don't know how I'm going to sleep knowing you're so close."

Josie grinned. "You're going to jack off and pass out in less than ten minutes. Don't try to play me."

Anders let out a loud laugh and cupped her jaw. "It sounded good though, right?"

"It sounded exactly like the bullshit it is."

Anders shrugged. "Can't blame a guy for trying."

"Never."

"Goodnight, Ivy," he whispered, placing a soft kiss on her lips.

"I'll meet you at the end of the aisle," she said. "I'll be the one in white."

"I'll be waiting." With a final sweet kiss, Josie slipped inside the villa and leaned against the closed door, her heart hammering in her chest. After a quick change of clothes, Josie, Lori, Chloe, Inky, and Maddie crawled into the oversized king bed, gossiping and laughing like they were in high school. When sleep finally pulled Josie under, her last thought was of seeing Anders waiting for her at the end of the aisle.

Chapter Nine

"WAKE UP, SLEEPING BEAUTY," MADDIE sang, tickling Josie's nose with the end of her hair. Josie batted her hand away.

"Come on, Josie. You're getting married today," Chloe giggled. Josie cracked a smile at that and opened her eyes slowly. Her two best friends hovered above her, their wide smiles causing Josie to let out a sleepy laugh.

"You guys have no respect for personal space."

"Didn't you make a bet about me having sex?" Inky asked. "Talk about invading personal space."

"In my defense," Josie said, sitting up in bed as all her friends circled her. "I bet that you'd hold out. Just saying."

Inky blinked. "Really? You saw his dick, right?"

Josie let out a loud laugh and tossed a pillow at Inky. "Does that mean I'm going to lose my money?"

Inky rolled her eyes. "Of course not. I just wanted to make sure you knew what I was up against."

"Or not against," Lori cut in.

"Okay, now that we've talked about Greer's dick for the fourth day in a row, how about we get this show on the road?" Chloe clapped her hands together and stood from the bed. "Go jump in the shower, Josie. We let you sleep in while we showered and dressed. Once you're done, we'll go have brunch then head to the spa."

Josie rolled out of bed with her stomach in her throat. She was getting married today. To Anders. Clearly, insanity ran in the family. After a quick shower, Josie piled her hair on top of her head and threw on a pair of loose shorts and a tank top. When she stepped out of the bathroom, her mom and Elizabeth had joined the group.

"Where's Abigail?"

Chloe rolled her eyes. "I have no idea. I've tried calling her several times. I have a key to her room. We can swing by and grab her on the way. She's probably sleeping off all those drinks she had last night."

"Your mom has put her liver to work this weekend," Maddie commented. Chloe nodded.

"She's going to need detox when she gets home."

Filing out of the villa, the group made their way toward Abigail's place, chatting and laughing about the night before. "This really has been an amazing trip. I'm so happy I got to have all of you here with me."

"I mean, you did pay for it," Inky joked. "We would have been idiots to say no."

"You really would have been," Josie laughed.

"Mom," Chloe yelled, banging her fist against the door. "We need to get going. Get up!" When there was no response, Chloe pushed in the keycard and opened the door. "Mom— Oh my God, Mom, what the fuck?"

The hysteria in Chloe's voice caused Josie's heart to leap in her chest. Pushing past Chloe, expecting to find a dead body or something, Josie stopped dead in her tracks. "Abigail!"

"That's the limbo guy from last night!" Inky gasped before

falling forward in a fit of laughter. "I can't breathe. Oh my God. This is amazing."

"It is not amazing," Chloe hissed, her hand covering her eyes.

Josie couldn't look away. She was pretty certain she was completely frozen. There in the bed was Abigail and, apparently, the limbo guy from the bonfire. And they were naked. In bed. Together.

"Why don't you girls head on to brunch? We'll catch up with you in a bit," Sonya said, her voice filled with amusement.

Chloe turned to Sonya and pointed at her mother. "She's not even sorry! Do you see that smile on her face? Do you see it? This is not okay!"

"Of course it is," Sonya said with a sly smile. "Maybe it's less okay that you happened to witness it firsthand, but it's still okay. Now, shoo. Elizabeth and I will be along soon."

Josie grabbed Chloe by the shoulders and guided her dumbstruck friend out into the fresh air. "Take a deep breath."

"I can't believe what I just saw," Chloe exhaled.

"So much for that wall," Inky said, still fighting to hold back her laughter.

"There's no wall. There's only my mother naked with a guy who is probably younger than me."

"At least he was hot," Lori offered, trying to find the silver lining.

Chloe inhaled deeply and turned toward Josie, her face apologetic. "Josie, I'm sorry, but I'm going to need a drink. I'm going to do my best to keep from getting drunk before your wedding. But right now, I just can't make any promises."

Josie let out a small laugh and looked at Maddie, who had been uncharacteristically quiet. "You okay there, Maddie?"

"Look, I've caught my parents in the act. I can't even fuck with her about this. It's next-level traumatizing." Maddie looked at Chloe. "Let's get you that drink. I'll make sure you don't stumble down the aisle."

"Thanks," Chloe mumbled, letting Josie lead her to the restaurant.

After ordering a round of Bloody Marys, mimosas, and a screwdriver with a splash of orange juice for Chloe, the girls settled into their seats and chatted while plates of food were brought to the table.

"You know, I never asked what you guys planned on doing for a honeymoon," Inky said, popping a piece of bacon into her mouth.

"Greece," Josie said with a smile. "It's going to be amazing."

Chloe sighed. "It's so beautiful. I told Reid we have to add it to our next tour and leave a few extra days for exploring."

"I concur," Inky said. "I love that I get to freeload off you guys and see the world."

"You do not freeload," Chloe argued. "You work just like the rest of us."

"I sell merchandise for the band. Not that I'm com-plaining—it's a great gig for me."

"I bet things will be a whole lot more interesting on this next tour," Maddie said, cutting her eyes to Inky.

Inky's expression was blank. "And why is that?"

"Don't be cute. I bet you and Greer are going to be worse than any of the stories you told us about Chloe and Reid."

Inky shook her head and let out an exasperated sigh. "You guys are going to have to let this thing with Greer go. It's unhealthy. It's also about as likely as Walker staying sober or

Owen developing a conscience. It's like fetch. It's never going to happen."

"Ladies," Abigail said, joining the group with Sonya and Elizabeth.

A look of relief washed over Inky's face, obviously expecting the conversation to shift to Abigail and Chloe, but Josie wasn't interested in more awkward conversation. In a matter of hours, she would be getting married, and her nerves were starting to take hold.

"I can't believe I'm getting married today," she said, noticing the slight tremble to her voice. It wasn't that she had doubts about her feelings for Anders or vice versa, but she was also realistic. Marriage was hard enough for normal couples, but for people like Anders, who lived their lives in the public eye, well, that added an extra level of stress.

"You're not having second thoughts, are you?" Sonya asked, her usual teasing demeanor absent.

"No," Josie said with a heavy exhale. "Just, what if Anders does? Not right now, but later down the road. What—"

"Stop," Abigail said, putting her hand on top of Josie's. "What-if is no way to live your life. If we all lived in fear of what might happen, then we'd never allow ourselves to experience any of the amazing, exciting things life has to offer. From someone who has done just that for far too long, trust me when I say, embrace the now."

Josie wasn't sure why, but the excitement and regret she heard in Abigail's voice caused her throat to tighten. "Thanks."

"For what it's worth," Elizabeth said, "I've known Anders for a long time. If nothing else, he is the most stubborn human being on the planet. He's made up his mind about you, and nothing or no one will ever be able to change it. You're stuck with that man for the rest of your life. Good luck with that."

"You sure you've really thought this through?" Maddie joked, making everyone laugh.

Josie stood from the table. "He might be an asshole, but he's my asshole. Now, let's get this show on the road."

A flurry of activity followed over the next few hours. Josie, Maddie, and Chloe returned to the bridal villa where a crew had set up three stations for their hair and makeup. The rest of the girls spent the afternoon making sure the flowers were perfect and overseeing the setup for the reception. And of course, blocking Anders from his repeated attempts to sneak in to visit Josie.

"Here," Maddie said, passing a small box to Josie.

Josie took the box, a confused smile on her face. "What's this?"

Maddie shrugged. "Tradition."

Josie unwrapped the box and gasped. "What is this?" Josie picked up the dainty bracelet, covered in diamonds.

"Your something borrowed. It's my mom's. She wanted you to wear it."

Josie's eyes filled with tears, and she had a feeling it was the first of many times it would happen that day. "It's beautiful. Thank you."

"My turn," Chloe said, passing Josie an envelope. "Something new."

Josie pulled out the folded sheet of paper, her brows drawn together until understanding dawned on her and her hand flew to her mouth. "Chloe! What is this?"

"We wrote a song about you guys. It's going to be on our upcoming album with your permission."

"Holy shit, that's awesome," Maddie said, leaning closer to get a look at the title. "'Hollywood & Vine.' That's perfect."

Josie mouthed the words, her heart soaring and her stomach in free fall as her relationship with Anders came to life on the page in front of her. "I love it."

"You're going to ruin your makeup," Maddie laughed, wiping the tears from under her eyes. "Quick, give her the blue before we all have to start over with our makeup."

Before Josie could blink, lace and silk smacked her arm. She looked down at the blue garter and laughed. "You guys are so awesome. Thank you so much!"

"This last one is from your mom." Maddie tossed the little box into Josie's lap.

Josie opened the box, and a small, nostalgic smile spread across her face. "These belonged to my grandmother." She turned to box toward Maddie and Chloe, the tiny diamond stud earrings glinting in the sunlight coming through the window.

"Those are perfect."

A silence fell over the trio as the women behind them put the finishing touches on their hair. "It's time to get dressed, Josie," Maddie said with a wide smile.

"Oh my God, I'm so nervous," Josie laughed, her hands shaking. "Where's my mom?"

"She just texted me that she's on her way."

"Okay." Josie stood from the chair and released a shaky breath. "Let's do this."

Maddie and Chloe disappeared into the bathroom while Josie paced the room and waited for her mother. She was so lost in her thoughts that she didn't even hear her come into the room until she felt a light touch on her shoulder. She spun around, her eyes widening as she looked at her mother.

"Mom, you look beautiful." Sonya's hair was twisted up at the nape of her neck, and her knee-length green-and-gold dress was fitted and flared, accentuating all of her best features. The dress was a perfect complement to Chloe's and Maddie's dresses.

"Thanks, honey. Now, let's get you in that gorgeous dress."

Josie nodded, her excitement spiking when her mother pulled down the zipper of the garment bag and removed the dress. "It's so perfect." It was one-shouldered, with golden thread embroidered into the satin in circles and swirls. The bottom was a mix of gold and white flowers sewn in delicate lace. It was simple and breathtaking.

"Are you ready to see?" Sonya asked, fastening the final hook on the back of the dress.

"Yes," Josie answered, spinning around to the mirror. She didn't even recognize herself. Her hair was twisted around the sides and gathered at the base of her neck, tiny tendrils falling along her cheeks. Even though her makeup was natural, she looked otherworldly.

"You're glowing," Maddie said, stepping beside her. "You look beautiful."

"So do you. Both of you," she said when Chloe stepped into the room. Their forest-green satin dresses were the same color, but Josie had let them pick their own style.

"It's time to go," Sonya said as there was a knock at the door. "We'll head down to the beach and give you and your father a minute."

Josie hugged her mom and her best friends and waved as they left, her smile freezing when she saw her dad. He cleared his throat and blinked, but it did nothing to hide the shimmer of tears in his eyes.

"My little girl is all grown up," he said, his voice unsteady.

"Ah, Dad," Josie said, trying to rein in her own emotions. "You look very handsome."

Keith looked down at his tux and shook his head. "This thing is hot as hell. This ceremony better not take long, or you're going to have a smelly bunch of guests."

Josie let out a loud laugh and hugged her dad. "Short and sweet. I promise."

He grumbled something else under his breath that Josie couldn't quite make out before holding out his arm for Josie to take. "You sure you want to marry this clown? You know Barry James still carries a torch for you. Nice kid."

"Barry James from middle school? The boy who threw up on me in the cafeteria while trying to ask me to the spring dance?"

Keith shrugged, his lip twitching. "You made him nervous."

"Yeah, I think I'll stick with Anders. I prefer a guy who doesn't puke on me."

"You never were one to take the easy way."

Josie laughed. With that, she couldn't disagree.

The music floated through the air, mixing with the calming sounds of the wind and water rolling onto the beach. The sun hung on the horizon, a fiery burst of red and orange caressing the sky. A large arbor covered in flowers with vines twisted through lattice sat atop a wooden platform. Flower petals covered the platform, and flickering candles lit the small path Josie would walk down with her father.

Anders stood next to the officiant, Holden and Reid to

his left. He cut his eyes to where Maddie and Chloe stood with wide smiles, their emotions written all over their faces. Gathered at the bottom of the platform, their friends and family chatted while they waited for Josie. When the music changed, Anders sucked in a sharp breath. The guests stood and turned, but Anders couldn't move a muscle.

"Jesus Christ," he exhaled, his mouth dry. He'd never seen anyone or anything more beautiful than the woman walking toward him. The moment their eyes connected, it was like all of the oxygen had been sucked out of the atmosphere. The hairs stood on the back of his neck, and a feeling of euphoria washed over him like he was floating. No person on earth had ever made him feel the way he did in that moment.

The officiant spoke, but it was like Anders was underwater, the voices around him garbled and indistinct. All he could see was Josie. His Ivy. Then she was standing next to him, and the air felt electrified. He reached out and cradled her jaw, his thumb sweeping across her cheek.

"Josie," he whispered, stepping closer, the world around them melting away.

"Hi," she breathed, her eyes glistening, her smile wide.

His entire body relaxed at her single word. He smiled back, the world slowly coming into focus. "Hey," he chuckled. "You're so beautiful."

"You don't look so bad yourself." Josie clutched her flowers to her chest and sucked her bottom lip between her teeth. "You ready to do this?"

"Abso-fucking-lutely."

"Anders!" Josie giggled, her eyes cutting to the officiant, who didn't seem the least bit surprised. After a moment, the officiant cleared his throat and looked between the pair before speaking.

"Welcome, family and friends. We are here today to celebrate the union of Anders and Josie. Each of you is here to offer your love and support to them along their journey through life together. Marriage is a commitment of the highest level, and your presence today, your blessing, encouragement, and lifelong support for their union means the world to them.

"Anders, Josie, marriage is the promise between two people who love each other, trust

that love, and honor one another as individuals. It enables two separate souls to share desires, dreams, joys, and sorrows. It's having a partner by your side through the uncertainties of life. A strong marriage allows you to maintain your unique identity and grow in your own way through the years ahead. It is a haven for each of you to become your best self, while together, you become better than you ever could be alone.

"Anders and Josie, please join hands, look at one another now, and remember this moment. When days are hard, when you feel you've reached the end of your rope, or time and complacency make you forget, think about this moment. Breathe in the emotions you feel right now. Remember the love, the fullness of your heart, the completeness of your soul standing next to each other, and hold on to that. Don't let it go. Remember, marriage is more than feelings. It's a decision. A promise. A lifelong commitment.

"Anders and Josie have written their own vows. Josie, you may say yours now."

"Okay," Josie exhaled, her voice breaking. "Anders, for the longest time, I thought there was something wrong with me. I remember thinking the reason I'd never felt any kind of spark with another person was because I was broken. Then I met you, and I realized there wasn't anything wrong with me—I was just waiting for you. You turned a spark into a raging inferno. You set me on fire in the best way. You make me feel things I never imagined. I promise to love you above all else. I promise to be there for you through the good and the bad. But most of all, I promise I will never break your heart. I will love you until my last breath, and even after that." The sweetest smile spread across her face as she blew out a heavy breath.

"Anders," the officiant said.

Anders licked his lips and shifted his weight. "Josie. Ivy," he said with a smile. "I look back on the last ten years of my life, the mistakes and bad decisions I've made, and I still can't believe where I am today. I never expected to change. Then I met you, and you turned my world upside down. Everything I thought I knew, everything I believed, was all wrong. You loved me for who I was, all my flaws, all my faults. You made me want to be a better man. You made me want to be worthy of your love. You made me love again when I never thought that would be possible. I'm not perfect, and I'm sure I'll do stuff that makes you want to bury me in the desert. But I promise to spend every day of the rest of my life making sure you know what you mean to me. I will love you until my last breath, and even after that."

Josie let out a breathy laugh when Anders winked. "Copycat," she mouthed. Anders shrugged. She wasn't the only one who could profess her undying love, dammit.

"Anders, do you take Josie to be your wife?"

"I do." Taking the ring from Holden, Anders slipped the gold band onto Josie's finger before lifting her hand and pressing a soft kiss just below the ring.

"Josie, do you take Anders to be your husband?"

"I do." With shaking hands, Josie slipped the wedding band onto Anders's finger as tears tracked down her cheeks. Anders felt like there was an iron vise around his lungs.

"Anders and Josie, you have come here today of your own free will and in the presence of family and friends to declare your love and commitment. You have given and received rings as the symbol of your promises. By the power of your love and commitment to each other, and by the power vested in me, I now pronounce you husband and wife. You may kiss the bride."

Anders smiled and stepped forward, cradling Josie's jaw and winding his fingers into her hair as he kissed her until they were breathless. Catcalls and cheers erupted from their friends and family as the pair broke apart. "Don't cry," Anders whispered, wiping a tear from under her eye.

"I'm just really happy."

"Me too, Ivy. I love you."

"I love you too."

"Friends and family, I now present to you Anders and Josie Ellis. Give them a hand!" Their friends and family continued to cheer as Anders and Josie rested their foreheads against one another, lost in each other's eyes.

Chapter Ten

HAND IN HAND, ANDERS AND Josie walked into the same room where they'd gathered three days earlier. This time, however, it was as husband and wife. Everyone cheered as they made their entrance, none louder than Walker.

"I see Walker is getting the party started early," Josie said with a smile.

Anders shook his head. "I don't think Walker's party ever stopped."

"Congrats, you two," Greer said, handing the pair glasses of champagne then looking at Anders. "You give hope to the rest of us sad assholes that we might get our shit together one day."

"Are you talking about anyone specifically, or is this a general statement?" Josie asked with a sly smile.

Greer narrowed his eyes. "You girls have been acting stranger than usual these last few days. What exactly is it you think you know?"

"Oh no," Anders said, pulling Josie's hand. "We are not having this conversation on my wedding day. Greer, thanks for the drink. But if you want answers, you'd better get them from someone else. Not today. No."

Josie let out a loud laugh as Anders dragged her away from a very confused Greer. "He's so clueless," Josie sighed.

"Can't say I don't get it. You did a real number on me."

Josie shrugged. "All I wanted was hot wall sex. You're the one who had to go and make this a lifetime commitment. You really messed up that whole one-night stand thing."

Anders pulled Josie against his chest, his expression disapproving. "Are you really going to bust my balls on our wedding day?"

Josie laughed. "Of course I am. Who do you think you're dealing with?"

Anders pursed his lips and narrowed his eyes. "So basically, everything is exactly the same as before, except you have a new ring and last name?"

Josie pretended to think about it before nodding. "Yeah. I guess so."

"As weird as it sounds, that makes me really fucking happy."

"Of course, it does," Josie said with a light laugh. "You'd be bored to tears if I didn't give you shit all the time."

"We're perfect for each other. You know that, right? There is no other person on this planet who would put up with either of our shit."

"That's what I'm counting on," Josie whispered. "Me and you forever and always."

"I couldn't imagine a single day of my life without you."

"Me either," Josie whispered before rolling up onto the balls of her feet and placing a soft kiss against Anders's cheek.

"Sorry to interrupt," Holden said, his face apologetic. "But these drinks are really strong, and Dad is worried he won't get his father-daughter dance if you guys don't do it now."

Josie and Anders looked around at their friends, their eyes widening as they realized just how drunk everyone was. "Jesus, we weren't gone that long taking pictures," Josie said. "What happened?"

Holden shrugged. "I have no idea, but I've switched to water and I still feel fucked up. Go have your dance so we can do the cake and shit."

"Got it," Josie laughed. The music changed, and Keith held out his hand to Josie as the familiar intro to "She's a Rainbow" by the Rolling Stones came on. "Dad," Josie laughed as he spun her around the dance floor.

"You're like a rainbow to me," Keith said with a smile. "Besides, your mother plans on having the mother-son dance with Anders. So we agreed to keep the songs upbeat, so she didn't act inappropriately."

"Oh my God," Josie giggled. "I hope Anders and I have the kind of relationship you guys have. You always have so much fun."

"She's my best friend, baby girl. Feelings ebb and flow where love is concerned, but friendship, well, that lasts forever. That's how we make things work. That's why I know you and Anders are going to make it. You have more than love. You have friendship."

"Thanks, Dad," Josie said, her eyes filling with tears.

"None of that now," he whispered, spinning her around. "You mother is about to drag Anders onto the dance floor. You need to be able to see this."

"Jesus," Josie laughed. "Does he even know?"

Keith looked to where Sonya was dragging a protesting Anders onto the dance floor. "He does now," he chuckled. As their song ended, Josie and her dad moved to the side as Tom Petty's "Mary Jane's Last Dance" began to play.

Josie lost it. "Mom chose a song about pot?"

"I can't control your mother. How have you not figured this out yet?"

Anders laughed and twirled Sonya around the dance floor, their friends dancing alongside them. Everyone clapped and cheered until the final note of the harmonica ended. Anders gave Sonya a kiss on the cheek and turned toward Josie.

He walked to her with purpose, extending his hand to her. "Are you ready for our dance?"

"Yeah. Did you pick it?"

"I did," he whispered, pulling her close as the opening of "Madness" by Muse flooded the speakers.

"You didn't," Josie exhaled with a smile.

"Can you think of a song that better fits us?"

"Not a one."

"Then dance with me."

They swayed to the hypnotic rhythms of the beat and the smooth sound of the lyrics. Anders brushed his thumb over Josie's cheek, the side of his mouth lifting into a soft smile when their eyes locked. "We really fucking did it."

Josie laughed and cupped her hand over his. "Having regrets already?"

"Fuck no," he answered before taking a slow look around the room. Everyone was completely hammered. "Why did we invite these people?"

Josie giggled. "Because they're our friends."

Anders quirked his brow. "Really? In the four days we've been here, I've been bruised, violated, almost set on fire, and exposed to things that even therapy can't help me cope with. All of this courtesy of our so-called friends."

Josie clamped her hand over her mouth, her shoulders

shaking with silent laughter. Anders narrowed his eyes and pursed his lips. "Go on, laugh it up."

Josie burst into a fit of giggles, the sound making Anders's chest tighten, even if her laughter was at his expense. "I'm sorry," she gasped, wiping under her eyes. "But aren't you exaggerating just a little bit?"

Anders blinked, his expression devoid of emotion. "Am I?"

Josie bit the inside of her cheek, a thoughtful expression taking over her features before she released a soft chuckle. "Okay, maybe you're not, but at least you didn't have to see that thing with Chloe's mom this morning. *That* was traumatic."

Anders grinned and pulled Josie against his chest as they continued to dance. "Aside from the trauma and almost dying, I guess it could've been worse."

"Really?"

"No," Anders conceded with a shake of his head. "It was a complete shitshow."

"It was the best."

Josie's stomach rumbled, and she looked toward their table. "Are you hungry?"

Anders smiled and held her in place even though the song had ended. "We have one more song."

"What—" Josie's words died in her throat as Reid and Chloe stepped onto the small stage.

"If I could have everyone's attention?" Reid asked, positioning his guitar as Chloe adjusted her violin. Neither looked all that steady on their feet. "We'd like to play a song we wrote for Anders and Josie."

"Did you know about this?" Josie asked, her eyes wide.

"Yeah, he played it for me today."

"I've read the lyrics, but I can't wait to hear it out loud."

"They did good."

Reid strummed his guitar, his eyes closed. After a moment, his voice floated across the room.

> *In the city of angels lives a devil with no disguise*
> *He plays the game, puts it all on the line*
> *No smoke and mirrors, he has nothing to hide*
> *Until Hollywood meets Vine*

Chloe played alongside him, their music in perfect harmony. When she began to sing, Josie's eyes filled with tears.

> *She wants him in ways she can't understand*
> *He sets her on fire with the touch of his hand*
> *But she knows his rules, how he can be cruel*
> *And she won't be taken for just another fool*

Reid took over again, his voice filled with emotions Anders understood all too well.

> *Different from the rest, she puts him to the test*
> *Won't let her in, won't let her go*
> *Thinks he running the show*
> *Little does he know, the whole thing is about to blow*

Together, Reid and Chloe sang the final verses, their voices rough and gentle, heavy and light. A perfect mixture of the love between Anders and Josie.

> *Love in the dark, lies in the light*
> *There are no winners in this fight*
> *When she walks away, they'll never be the same*
> *What starts as a game catches aflame*
> *And what they feel suddenly has a name*

They can't let go, can't move on
Their lives intertwined, they no longer hide
Hollywood and Vine
She holds him close, chases away the ghosts
He loves her like he should
Changes in ways he never thought he could
Their fate is sealed, it's a done deal
It's Hollywood and Vine, a love you can't define

Tears streamed down Josie's face as she hugged Anders close, lost in the final notes of their song. Reid and Chloe stepped off the stage to cheers and hugs as they made their way toward Anders and Josie.

"That was beautiful," Josie whispered, hugging Chloe then Reid.

"I'm glad you liked it," Chloe said, stumbling a bit.

Josie looked at Reid and narrowed her eyes. He had a ridiculous smile on his face and appeared to be hanging on to Chloe to keep his balance. "What the hell is wrong with you guys?"

Before Reid could respond, Abigail grabbed him and Chloe in a tight hug. "I'm so proud of you two," she gushed, causing Josie to take a step back.

"Oh boy," Josie whispered, taking Anders by the hand. "Let's go sit at our table. We should eat something before we end up like the rest of them." They made their way to the table as the music changed and everyone crowded onto the dance floor. Their friends moved in ways that made Josie cover her eyes.

"This won't end well," Anders said. Josie peeked through her fingers toward the dance floor.

Walker was dancing with Inky, his hands sliding toward

her ass. Anders and Josie were amazed she hadn't punched him in the dick.

"Here we go," Josie said, gripping Anders's hand. "At least the pictures are done." Greer walked to where Walker was groping Inky, but instead of Greer decking him as they'd both expected, Inky went airborne as Greer threw her over his shoulder and carried her out of the room, her angry words tempered by her fit of giggles.

"They've all lost their minds." Anders shook his head and reached for his glass, pausing when he noticed an old-looking bottle with a grass ribbon tied around the neck. "What's that?" Anders had a bad feeling.

"I don't know." Josie grabbed the small note taped to the mostly empty bottle, her brows drawing together as she read the note. "'Enjoy the special kava.' What does that mean?"

"Oh my fucking God," Anders whispered. "They did it again."

"Who did what? What are you talking about?"

Anders grabbed the bottle of liquid and walked to the window, pouring out the contents. "Remember the village by the cave? What happened there?"

Understanding washed over Josie's face. "No…"

"Yes. All these fuckers are tripping on shrooms. On the bright side, they'll be fine in about three hours."

"Anders, why would they do this?"

"Do you guys like my surprise?" Walker asked, his smile a million miles wide.

Anders narrowed his eyes. "What did you do?"

"I got a bottle of booze from the village we visited. I thought you'd like it."

"What exactly did you ask for?" Anders asked through clenched teeth.

Walker squinted and wobbled a bit. "I just asked for something good for a wedding reception. This is what they sent."

"Jesus," Anders said under his breath. "Walker, they gave you shroom juice. Again. Do you remember what happened last time?"

Walker blinked once then twice before his face went slack. "Oh shit. I fucked up. Maybe I really should go to a real rehab next time."

"Should we tell anyone?" Josie whispered.

Anders shook his head. "At this point, I think we should just let it go."

"I can't believe this is happening."

"You know what would make it better?" Anders asked, his eyes flicking to the hall.

Josie lifted her head, her smile widening. "You're relentless." He was never going to stop asking for wall sex.

"Come on. No one will even miss us. Look at them." Josie looked around the room; everyone was high as a kite. Anders saw the exact moment she caved.

"Come on, Ivy. Let's consummate this marriage." He tugged on her hand, and they slipped out of the room and down the low-lit hallway. Anders twisted the knob to the office door, his smile widening as he pushed it open.

"Hurry up," Josie whispered, pushing him into the room before locking the door behind her.

Surrounded by darkness, Anders wasted no time putting his lips to her skin. He wanted to taste every inch of her before stripping her down and fucking her against the wall just like he'd done the first time they'd met. Only this time, she wasn't a random hookup. She was his wife. The thought made him groan as he cupped her ass and rocked his hips against her.

"Ivy…"

"Shit!"

Anders jumped and Josie screamed as the sound of another voice came from the back of the room. Something crashed to the floor as a masculine voice let out a string of swears. Anders fumbled for the light switch, his jaw tight.

"Who the hell is in here?"

As soon as light flooded the room, Josie gasped and covered her mouth, while Anders shook his head. From the moment they'd stepped foot on the island, it had been one surprise after another. But for once, Anders wasn't surprised at all.

"Told you," he muttered, cutting his eyes to Josie, but she wasn't looking at him. She stretched out her arm and pointed toward the other side of the room. "You were supposed to hold out," she said, her shoulders shaking with laughter.

"You owe me twenty bucks," Anders gloated.

"Don't be so cocky. I might owe you twenty bucks, but they just cockblocked our wall sex."

Anders looked from Josie to Greer and Inky, who were still fumbling for their clothes. His annoyance transformed into mischief. "Like hell they did. They're going to leave. Right now."

"They're not really decent," Josie chuckled.

"We won't be either in less than a minute."

Josie's eyes widened as she understood what Anders was about to have them do. Stepping to the side, she smiled and opened the door.

"I thought we were friends, Josie," Inky whined, fixing the strap on her dress. Not that it mattered. They could be completely dressed, and what they'd just been doing would still be the most obvious thing in the world.

Josie leaned into Anders's side and grinned. "Of course we are. Now, go. It's your turn to be the stars of this shitshow."

As soon as they'd cleared the doorway, Anders slammed the door as Josie gasped for air between bouts of laughter. A moment later, cheers and catcalls echoed from the reception hall, Maddie's voice heard above all the rest. "I knew it!" she yelled. "I win!"

"Serves them right."

"You're just mad about the money," Anders teased.

"Among other things," Josie whispered, wrapping her hand around Anders's tie and pulling him toward the wall. "Now, where were we?"

A smile broke across Anders's face before he leaned forward and pressed his lips to hers. "I'm about to fuck you against this wall, Mrs. Ellis."

"God, I love the sound of that," Josie moaned.

"And I love you."

"Until my last breath, and even after that."

Anders wrapped his hands in her hair, their eyes locked with an intensity that sucked the air from the room. "And even after that," he promised.

Acknowledgements

To my husband Mark, thank you for not killing me for setting insane deadlines and dragging you into mt crazy book world.

Jennifer—Thank you for persuading me to set the crazy deadline mentioned above. Honestly, I don't know that I would have completed this project without your "encouragement" aka giant shove in the back!

Mia—Thank you for always sticking with me, pushing, and supporting my writing. I honestly can't imagine where I would be without you in my life. Thank you for indulging every facet of my craziness on a daily basis.

Julie—Thank you for dropping everything to read this for me even though you have two tiny people at home that keep you running twenty-four hours a day. You always make time for me and it means so much.

Kelly—Thank you for having the most ridiculous conversations with me, many of which end up in my books. Stay crazy, my friend.

Christine—Thank you for being my friend and cheerleader! Talking with you always makes me feel better.

Jada—At this point, I don't know why I should be surprised at how amazing my covers look. You did it again, and in record time!

Lisa—My wonderful editor, we did it again. Thank you for staying cool, calm, and collected when I dropped this manuscript in your lap with the dumbest deadline ever and you were like, "we've got this." I can't imagine anyone else ever editing my words. Also, I promise to try to not do this again. Please note the word try for future reference. ILY!

Jill—Thank you for jumping on the bandwagon of crazy and helping me turn this hot mess into a well formatted, albeit still, hot mess. You are part of this team and I couldn't do this without you.

And last but certainly not least, to my girls, my "Entourage". If people know about my books, it's likely because of y'all. The tweets, the shares, the out and out balls to the wall pimping that you all do is mind blowing. Thank you for taking time out of your busy lives to spread the word about my books. You guys are the best ever.

To everyone who takes the time to read my words, thank you. There are millions of books out there, thanks for choosing mine. Without you, none of this would be possible.

About the Author

Olivia Evans is a dreamer by day, writer by night. She's obsessed with music and loves discovering new bands. Traveling the world and watching the sun set in every time zone sounds like heaven to her. A true Gemini, she follows her heart blindly and lives life to the fullest with her husband, son, and friends. Her other loves are: Chuck Taylors, Doc Martens, concert tees, gangster movies, sports, wine, craft beer, and her shih tzu babies.

Connect with Olivia on Facebook, Goodreads, Instagram, or visit her website at www.oliviaevansauthor.com.

Other Titles by Olivia Evans
Hollywood & Vine
Brooklyn & Beale
Flutter